Wolf's Bane

Moon Marked, Volume 1

Aimee Easterling

Published by Wetknee Books, 2018.

WOLF'S BANE

First edition. June 11, 2018.

Copyright © 2018 Aimee Easterling.

ISBN: 1720804265

Written by Aimee Easterling.

Chapter 1

The first time my mother spoke to me from beyond the grave, my little sister was defying gravity.

"The nail that sticks out gets hammered down," the disembodied voice of my dead mother noted inside my head just as a very real Kira called out: "Look, Mai! I'm flying!"

Jolting at Mama's unexpected intrusion, I swiveled to take in my sister's long legs scampering atop the six-foot high-wall at the edge of the cemetery. I usually didn't pay much attention to Kira's affinity for gymnastics in high places. But it wasn't every day a long-dead Japanese woman tapped on the inside of my skull and demanded that I take notice.

So—"Careful!" I called just as Kira's right foot touched down on a section of wall where the weight of the hillside had pushed the cinder blocks out at an angle, ivy and dirt promising to send the unwary tumbling off her stride.

"I know what I'm doing!" my sister replied, tossing her head and rolling her eyes just like she'd done yesterday and the day before and the day before that while walking home from school. All the while human feet pranced through the debris with the agility of a fox, proving that she was right and I was wrong. My concern—and the warning from our dead mother—had been for nothing.

Or so it seemed until my sister raised her chin toward the surprisingly bright March sunshine, closed her eyes to better soak up the warmth...and ran smack dab into the largest male body I'd seen in my life.

A moment earlier, I could have sworn that the cemetery—or at least what I could see of it from the recessed sidewalk—was entirely devoid of life. But now my little sister's shoulders were caught in the grip of hands that could oh-so-easily slide upward to settle around her unprotected neck. Veins stood out from the assailant's rippling muscles. And I didn't need to lift my nose to the breeze to understand what had taken place.

Kira had been waylaid by our worst possible enemy—an alpha male werewolf.

FOR HALF A SECOND, they wobbled there together atop tilting chunks of concrete. One girl who hid a secret punishable by death. And one predator who was willing and able to perform said execution.

Beneath them, I clenched my fist around the strobing ball of light shielded by the fabric of my pants pocket while at the same time assessing possible approaches. The trouble was, while I *could* jump directly onto the wall from my current location, doing so would be royally stupid within view of an alpha werewolf. But ascending in a human manner would mean running halfway down the block to the gateway Kira had so agilely leapt across...while leaving my sister unprotected in the interim.

So I stood for one endless second mimicking a stranded fish, mouth gaping and metaphorical fins flapping while I tried to decide which approach was least likely to get my sister killed. Meanwhile, beneath my clothes, the incorporeal light that held half my soul oozed out of my pocket, slid around my hip, and slowed at last in the empty scabbard strapped to my back. There the ice-cold tendrils of my star ball lengthened and solidified into my favorite weapon—a rapier-thin sword, just waiting to be drawn and wielded against the unwary.

The entire magical manipulation—plus associated brain freeze—had taken only a second, one blink of the eye during which my sister's assailant didn't appear to notice he had any audience other than one twelve-year-old child. His slender fingers had neither loosened nor tightened, and he spoke now in a voice so deep it was dangerous. "Someone's hunting innocents in this city. You shouldn't be out here alone."

Half of my brain occupied itself assessing that assertion. Was this werewolf—the most hazardous being we could possibly run up against—honestly warning my kid sister to steer clear of other predators? Or was that a threat half hidden beneath the throaty timbre of his overtly protective words?

But most of my attention remained focused on planning out my subsequent actions. I couldn't toss the sword to Kira and risk her being cut on an edged weapon, not when the twelve-year-old still used training blades in the school gymnasium where I taught. And was it even a good idea to provide a weapon in the first place when anything I threw upwards could just as easily end up in the lightning-quick hands of an overpowering alpha?

While other possibilities flicked through my brain with the force of strobe lights, Kira answered back as airily as if she and this werewolf were chance-met friends chatting during a stroll through the park. "Oh, I'm not alone," she said blithely. "I've got Mai."

"Your what?"

"No, not 'my.' *Mai.*"

Which is when I decided that running up the three-inch-wide staircase created by the cracking wall was *almost* easy enough to appear human. After all, the werewolf's fingers remained poised inches away from my sister's jugular. Didn't Kira realize that a being so powerful inevitably thought anything he could hold onto was his to keep?

So, relinquishing all concern about appearing human, I took the first two steps up the side of the wall in one lunging leap. Then I froze as the male's chin tilted down toward me.

His eyes were windows I was unprepared to gaze into. Piercing and assessing and, at the same time, as deep and full of mystery as the bottom of a well. He quirked arching eyebrows, the faintest hints of crows' feet appearing at his temples...only to fade as he took in the rapier I'd unconsciously extended to prod against his jeans-clad calf.

"Ah, I see," the male answered. "You *are* quite admirably protected. My mistake."

Then, without so much as nudging the sharpened steel away from his flesh, the werewolf released my sister's shoulders and offered me a perfunctory half-bow. He was as lithe as a swordsman, his body as perfectly proportioned as a statue hailing from ancient Greece.

"It's a pleasure to meet you, Mai." And to my sister—"Mind your balance, child." With that parting shot, the werewolf slid back out of my sight line, disappearing into the cemetery as quickly as he'd materialized in the first place.

And me? I was left with a hint of sweetness on my lips that reminded me of near-forgotten teenage kisses. Swiping one hand across my mouth to remove the tell-tale flavor, I jerked my chin at my sister. "We need to get you home."

After all, my second job was calling. Cage fights wait for no woman.

Chapter 2

I wouldn't dream of heading into battle without my black leather jacket and knee-high boots, but there was more to this gig than fighting. So I showed up at the Arena an hour later in a baby-pink blouse, ruffled neckline drooping low enough to show off my nearly nonexistent boobs. I tied up my hair in two above-the-ear pigtails. And I splashed enough smoky blue and silver eye shadow on either side of my nose to accentuate the slant of my half-Japanese eyes.

The effect wasn't me...but I'd do a lot to put food on the table for my sister. In this case, unfortunately, a lot wasn't quite enough.

"...did you hear about the hooker they found dead down by the river last week..."

"...new bar with two-for-one appetizers..."

"...wouldn't bet against Mai if you paid me to..."

The news of the day swirled around me in a cloud of horrors, excitement, and—unfortunately—overwhelming appreciation for my prowess. As if to prove the last point, a meaty hand came down on my shoulder as a random audience member congratulated me on my most recent win. "Nice job against those bozos," he boomed.

The male in question was a head and shoulders taller than my five-feet-zero frame, and he likely could have lifted me off the ground with one arm tied behind his back. Still, his posture radiated respect for more than the length of my rapier...which *should* have filled me with much-deserved pride.

Unfortunately, my boss had been using the unlikely disconnect between my appearance and my skill level to her financial advantage for nearly a decade. It was a lucrative proposition—toss the tiny street girl out against a gang of heavy hitters, bet on the underdog, and watch the cash roll in. Since my ten percent of the take paid the rent, having members of the audience betting *for* me rather than against me could very well turn into a financial disaster for both Ma and myself.

Drat and blast! What did it take to be underestimated in this town?

Before I could decide which evasive action to take, though, I glanced toward the other side of the stadium where my opponents usually held court. Best to see what kind of warrior Ma Scrubbs had dug up before I decided between the damsel-in-distress routine and the fake-wound walk....

New fighters were always easy to pick out due to the contestants' banners slung across their chests. And I was ready for any number of them. After all, I'd faced down five opponents just last month, forgetting myself and knocking the quintet down like dominoes with a few short swipes of my sword.

But during that ill-matched contest, I hadn't been forced to hide my abilities. Had been facing humans only, without a single werewolf in sight.

Now, as I eyed one tall male and one erect-ruffed four-legger, I not only recognized the abilities of the shifters before me, I also knew immediately who they were. The man standing on two legs possessed uncannily familiar features for all that

I'd never set eyes on his face before. And no wonder when he smelled identical to the wolf panting by his side, both boasting the same deep musk that lingered on my tongue despite every effort to wash their granite and ozone signature out of my brain.

No, these opponents weren't strangers. Or at least the wolf wasn't. Instead, this was the self-same shifter who had accosted my sister on the cemetery wall earlier in the afternoon.

Meanwhile, the two-legged shifter's words were just barely audible with the help of my own supernaturally assisted hearing. "Of course this is a good idea," the male murmured on the other side of the chattering crowd. His voice was gritty with rebellion, which struck me as strange since I could smell his dominance from fifty feet distant. "You know the evidence leads here."

Evidence? Were these werewolves hunting something? Could they possibly be seeking *me*?

Whether that conclusion was grounded in reality or in pure paranoia, I'd risk too much by fighting fellow shifters unaware of my closely held secret. So I turned on my heel and stalked off in the opposite direction.

It was time to hold a serious conversation with my boss.

"YOU'RE LATE."

Ma Scrubbs glowered at me across a table littered with dollar bills and scraps of hastily scrawled wagers. To the uninitiated, the mess looked like, well, a *mess*. But my second-shift supervisor memorized each offering, constantly recalculated the odds, and ensured the finances fell forever in her favor.

Not so difficult when she had a fighter like me in her back pocket.

Which, tonight, she most definitely did *not*. "I'm not doing it, Ma," I responded, slamming the door of my employer's office to block out the crowd so I could transition from Disney princess into hardened warrior and feel like myself once again. Only after stuffing both arms into the leather jacket waiting for me on the back of the door then buttoning the armor up to my chin did my heart calm sufficiently for me to fall into the empty seat waiting on the other side of Ma's desk.

"Cool it with the tantrums, girlie. And I'm not your mother. So don't call me 'Ma.'" As she spoke, the older woman's brows scrunched together into a glower that I was far too familiar with. Because, no, Ma Scrubbs wasn't my mother. But she'd let me play in her office dozens of times while my father fought, had offered me his vacated spot when I struggled to keep my tiny family afloat after being orphaned at age eighteen, and was the closest thing to a parental figure I had left.

So I obeyed her command and elaborated as best I could without mentioning supernatural elements that Ma Scrubbs may or may not have picked up on by now. "I can't win against those two," I explained. "It's just not possible. Pick someone else for the first fight then I'll go in for round two."

Ma Scrubbs considered me from the far side of the desktop, her head barely visible above the cluttered surface. If I was small, she was wizened, face so wrinkled it was impossible to guess what the seventy-year-old might have looked like when she was young. After a moment of consideration, she shrugged, pulling a battered notebook out of one pocket. "Go home then," she told me. "I'll call the Raven sisters in to fight."

"No!" The word burst from my lips before I could soften the rejection. "They're children! They'll be slaughtered!"

"Not against those two. Gunner and Ransom are boy scouts. First blood will be a nick on the cheek. Won't even scar. And next week, ticket sales will skyrocket out of sight."

So she *was* aware of the existence of werewolves. No human would refer to a four-legged shifter in the same breath as his two-legged companion unless she fully understood the former's ability to change forms.

Still, I had no time to further analyze that fact because Ma Scrubbs wasn't even looking at me any longer. Instead, she pulled out her cell phone and began thumbing through her address book, stopping only when the faces of Jessie and Charlie Raven popped into view. The twins were sweet young things who I'd mentored for a couple of summers. Despite my best efforts, though, the duo still thought fencing was a sport in which you didn't hit below the belt or above the neck. They had no concept werewolves existed and they were barely older than my kid sister. If I didn't allow Kira to sit in the Arena's audience, I certainly wasn't going to be responsible for Jessie and Charlie ending up within the Arena's cage.

So even though I knew I was being played, I reached out and blocked the phone's surface with my hand. "Okay, you win," I answered. Took a deep breath, considered the angles. I couldn't use my supernatural speed to its full advantage against a pair of werewolves, but there had to be a way to turn my opponents' cockiness against them.

If there was, Ma Scrubbs surely would have thought of it. "And you clearly have a plan," I continued. "So let's hear it."

"It's simple," my boss answered, her eyes twinkling with old-lady mirth. "You've been winning, winning, always winning. Nobody's gonna bet against you. So tonight, you'll reset the clock. Tonight...you'll lose."

Chapter 3

Losing, unfortunately, wasn't as easy as I'd expected. Oh, sure, when the cage door clanged shut, leaving me trapped within a small chain-link enclosure with two very large werewolves, the shiver running down my spine suggested the hard part would be merely staying alive. But my opponents—for all that they appeared to be brothers—combined to create the worst team imaginable.

Ransom—the human-form brother and the only one the announcer had introduced by name—turned out to be a run-of-the-mill opponent. He was fast and aggressive and out for my blood.

His brother, on the other hand, was not.

"Get out of my way!" Ransom muttered between gritted teeth the third time Gunner tangled himself between his sibling's legs and made it nearly impossible for the human sibling to dodge my blows...let alone get in one of his own. I would have laughed out loud if my goal hadn't been to lose the match subtly enough so the audience wouldn't wring my neck afterwards. As it was, my cheeks heated with frustration and I could almost feel next month's rent money slipping out of my grasp.

Meanwhile, the crowd was no more pleased than I was at my opponents' inability to put up a passable show. "Boo!" howled one angry bystander while fingers rattled the cage inches from my head. A beer bottle cleared the fence and shattered onto the mat a yard away from my booted feet, the glass shards turning into makeshift blades my opponents could pick up at any moment and use against my flesh.

In the midst of all this mayhem, I needed to not only survive but also to lose without appearing to throw over the fight. Time to implement my favorite weapon—my tongue.

"Ma Scrubbs told me you two were boy scouts," I said conversationally even as I danced through a series of warm-up exercises that appeared far more impressive than they really were. Had to keep the crowd happy while gearing up for the grand finale. "I'm thinking you look more like Brownies, though. Or maybe Daisies. Did you even earn enough merit badges to sell Girl Scout cookies yet?"

In response, Ransom growled between human teeth and took a single step forward, but I could have sworn Gunner was amused rather than provoked by my taunts. Whatever the reason, the latter's lupine jaws gaped open, his tongue lolling off to one side even as he blocked his brother as gracefully as if the two were dancing a minuet.

You-fight-like-a-girl jabs clearly weren't going to move this match along to the point where the audience would go home happy. So I assessed the way the two males worked in effort-filled non-harmony. Guessed reasons why one gamecock brother might choose to engage in battle while the other would undermine Ransom's authority at every turn...while still insisting upon guarding his sibling's back.

Then I opened my mouth and launched a second attack. "New alpha can't handle his own fights, can he?" I guessed, piecing together whispers I'd recently heard emerging from the few shifters I dared to speak with. "Just another dumb jock inheriting shoes too big for his puny feet. You know what they say about a guy with small feet...."

And just like that, the brothers glanced at each other in perfect harmony. Silent words streaked between them while the scents of fur and electricity filled the air.

At last, I'd gotten under their skins.

How like wolves to get riled up over issues of heredity...and shoe size. I let a smile crinkle my cheeks for a split second, but then it was time for battle.

Because both brothers were leaping toward me in synchronized splendor now. And above our heads, a surge of approval rolled out over the crowd.

FOR LONG SECONDS, MY world narrowed down to the simplicity of attack and parry. I hooked the hilt of my sword around one of Ransom's knives and pulled it out of his grip as easily as I disarmed raw beginners in my day job. But with Gunner circling slyly toward my blind spot, I was soon forced onto the defensive, spinning on my back foot and stabbing wildly to force the wolf into a retreat.

Whoosh. My sword cut deeper toward my lupine opponent than I'd intended, and I held my breath as hairs sprayed out around us both. If I'd misjudged my reach and pricked Gunner's skin, the match would be over before it really started...and not in a way that would please my picky boss.

Rent, I reminded myself as I scrambled backwards, glad there was no blood welling up where my blade had recently made contact with the four-legged werewolf. *Groceries. Bus money. More magic-trick paraphernalia for Kira's birthday next week. Tuition at her school in the nice part of town....*

Gradually, the roar of the crowd receded into the background and calm descended upon me just as it did every day during training. I grabbed the veil of control Dad had taught me to wield two decades earlier, slowed my attacks and parries until they matched my gasping breaths. *There.* The outer world meant nothing. Now I could be certain my blade would fly eternally true.

"I know what you are."

And to my eternal embarrassment, I stumbled, Ransom's words cutting through my hard-earned concentration far more admirably than my earlier verbal parry had interrupted his. The pack leader's knowledge of my identity was impossible. Because if werewolves were aware of my family's secret, their leader wouldn't be fighting me in a cage match. The whole pack would instead descend upon Kira and me as a unit, intent upon tearing out both of our throats.

As I tried to make sense of the nonsensical, Ransom took advantage of my turmoil. Swiping his sole remaining knife beneath my armpit, he opened up a nick in the jacket that had protected me year after year. And even though the cut didn't reach all the way to my skin, I was so shaken by the damage that I took a step backward...

...and promptly stumbled over Gunner, who'd poised himself in just the right spot to take advantage of my lapse. I teetered, nearly falling. Then I decided not to fight the imminent collapse. Instead, I allowed the accidental momentum to propel me sideways as I slashed my sword in a Z pattern in front of the unruly wolf's nose.

The sword-waving warning gave me breathing room to come up behind the two-legger's unguarded back. And, okay, so maybe I called upon a little supernatural speed to get me there. Maybe I bent my sword slightly away from its target so the metal didn't come in contact with game-ending flesh. But, in the midst of combat, who would either know or care?

The sharp tang of success cleared my head the way it always did. And I realized as I set up the defeat I so badly needed that my opponent was merely accusing me of being an unaffiliated werewolf...not of something considerably worse. After all, I smelled as much like fur as the brothers with whom I shared the stage at the moment. And more than a century since our supposed eradication, most shifters probably didn't believe beings like myself and my sister continued to exist.

So I ran with it. "Yep, you're right. I'm outpack. That means I don't have to kowtow to the new alpha who thinks his farts don't stink," I bantered, knowing that my voice would prompt Ransom's body to swivel just the way I wanted it to. Knowing that his knife would spin through the air at precisely the same level as the hand I'd raised in supposed self-defense. The sharp blade would cut through the flesh of my palm deeper than the scratch Ma Scrubbs had promised these boy scouts would dole out in victory, but the searing pain was more than worth the result.

Because as red blood dripped toward the ground between us, the audience erupted into jubilation. They'd lost their hard-earned money on the match, but they'd enjoyed every minute of the tussle that had come before this bitter end. The crowd would be even larger next week...and in the meantime I'd take home a rather hefty ten percent for my surprise upset.

"Good fight," Ransom offered, holding out a hand to shake without any arrogance in his posture at all. He really was a boy scout. As gentlemanly in his win as he would have been after a loss.

"Good fight," I agreed, swapping the sword over to my bloody left hand so I could return the hand clasp. Only then did I turn toward Gunner and shiver as something darkly suspicious flickered behind sienna lupine eyes.

Maybe my lapses hadn't been quite as overlookable as I'd thought in the heat of the moment. Now, I decided, would be a good time to beat a hasty retreat.

Chapter 4

I lost myself in the crowd before Gunner could shift and find me. Nodded at a bouncer then slipped through a heavy fire door to enter the private hallway that led toward the quiet of my personal changing room. I was ready for thirty minutes of down time before returning home to my sleeping sister. Thirty minutes to relax while Ma Scrubbs counted dollars and divvied up my share of the take.

Unfortunately, there was a werewolf on the couch when I thrust the door open. And not just any werewolf, but the one who thought he ran the city I lived within.

"My dear," Jackal greeted me, remaining recumbent for one long moment before unfolding long limbs and springing gracefully to his feet. He wore a half-unbuttoned silk shirt that showed off hardened muscles and his hair curled dashingly over both ears. Despite the eye candy, though, my attention remained firmly focused upon the promised respite of the couch behind his back.

There should have been overtures to live through before I could achieve my destination, but lack of nearby underlings put a kibosh on our customary embrace. Instead, Jackal merely raised his eyebrows and waited until I'd sunk into the leathery cushions before taking the opposite end of the sofa and getting straight to the point.

"Two Atwoods in my city." In front of the drifters who made up his not-quite-pack, Jackal would have donned a mask of alpha invulnerability. But the understanding between the two of us was sufficient to prevent him from mincing words. As a result, his observation came out as less of an observation and more of a pout.

I shrugged, wishing for one split second that Jackal really was my significant other. The pretense propped up Jackal's alpha tendencies in public and protected me and my sister when we walked through the city alone. A mutually beneficial arrangement...but one that, unfortunately, left me without anyone to rub my weary feet.

Perhaps that's why my subsequent words came out harsher than I'd intended. "In *their* city," I countered. "The pack leaders might not have been around much lately, but technically it's Atwood land for another hundred miles south."

Which was entirely true. But apparently I'd gone a step too far in reminding Jackal that he was poaching on a more established clan's territory while lacking sufficient manpower to back up his claim.

"*I'm* the one who keeps this city stable. *I'm* the one who keeps you safe," my companion bit out, a droplet of spittle striking my jacket while his fist came down to pound the leather cushion an inch from my thigh.

Yep, I should have stopped while I was ahead. Accepting my own misstep, I attempted to fix the faux pas with a little male ego-stroking. "You're right," I agreed. "But the brothers are just passing through. They're probably scouting the edges of clan territory, getting their bearings. After all, their father just recently died."

I expected Jackal to relax back onto the cushions, to accept what he couldn't change. But instead, something dark and menacing rose within his eyes, and his muscles tensed with lupine alertness when next he spoke.

"Well, they'd better keep moving," he told me. "Because this city and everything in it is *mine*."

"BE CAREFUL OUT THERE," Ma Scrubbs warned as she led me to the back door half an hour later. The old woman had been alerting me about the city's hidden dangers ever since I'd started trailing along behind my father two decades earlier. But something in my employer's tone promised a rapier might not be enough to keep my skin intact tonight.

Still, I had a hard time taking the threat seriously when my pockets were full of cash and all three werewolves I'd run into this evening were long gone through the opposite entrance. So I offered a jaunty salute and strode away into the darkness, already counting the moments until I could fall into my warm bed. Just one last stop at the corner store for bread and milk to ensure Kira's cheery disposition, then I could rest easy in the knowledge that I'd raked in sufficient supplemental income to ensure our survival for another week at least....

Or so I thought for the few minutes it took to exit the Arena's alley and turn onto the wide but quiet avenue that formed the main artery of this part of town. Only after enough time had passed that Ma Scrubbs would have removed her hearing aids and descended into her basement apartment did a thread of sound cut through my thoughts of hearth and home.

And at first, I thought the auditory intrusion was merely a run-of-the-mill wolf whistle. But I couldn't make out a single human shape lingering in the shadowed doorsteps I was passing. And this sound was less a whistle and more a thread of barely discernible melody that sent a trickle of prey-like awareness skittering up my spine.

As much as I strained, though, I couldn't make sense of the disjointed notes. The night musician was quite a distance behind me, I estimated. Perhaps a block or two east as well....

But then the tones coalesced into a strangely familiar lullaby, the tune popping to life as if emerging from a dully remembered childhood. And even though my curiosity was piqued by the vague memory, my gut told me the sound represented danger rather than intrigue. So I sped up my footsteps, wishing I hadn't already shrunken my magical star ball away from its sword shape and down into its easy-to-carry energetic form. Now would be a good time to be holding onto a blade....

Even another human on the streets would have been appreciated at the present moment. Anything to jolt away the adrenaline-rush of terror that was flooding my body for no discernible reason. Was I really about to break into a sprint to escape from a *song*?

Unfortunately, the streets on every side of me were dark and empty. And the whistle continued at exactly the same volume even as I sped up my pace, as if my follower had increased his own footsteps in synchrony rather than falling behind as I would have hoped.

Yes, the tune's volume remained steady...but its tempo gradually lessened until both my star ball and my feet were pulsing in sympathy. Like Kira, I enjoyed moving quickly and silently. But now my instinctive press for speed felt akin to slogging through a sea of molasses. Meanwhile, my boots thudded against the pavement with every descending step.

What's wrong with me? Stifling a shiver, I glanced backwards, half expecting a fairy-tale monster to be following in my wake....

But my gaze met with nothing out of the ordinary. Just the usual potholed pavement, one streetlight vainly attempting to illuminate an entire block. Doors were locked, windows were grimed over, and a single rat was the only living being in sight.

There *was* light ahead of me though. The 7-Eleven came into view like an oasis in a desert, the brightest patch of safety around.

And sure, the establishment possessed grease-stained windows along with an air of declining profitability. But I knew from experience that the store also boasted a rifle-toting clerk and a back door that would spit me out into an untraveled alley. If necessary, the clerk would cover my back sufficiently so I could use my hidden abilities in safety, then I could slink home with my tail quite literally between my legs.

Or maybe I'd get lucky and my stalker would turn out to be a cheerful passerby who whistled his way past the plate-glass windows without so much as a glance in my direction. Kira could enjoy milk on her morning cereal with toast as a chaser, and all would be right in our little world.

Still, I flung open the 7-Eleven door with my head turned in search of my pursuer...and had no warning as I ran smack dab into a far too familiar chest.

Chapter 5

"You and your sister don't look where you're going very often, do you?"

Gunner's fingers burned against my wrist as he restrained me from...what? Pulling a sword that didn't currently exist? Punching him in the eye or kneeing his balls in an effort to relax his grip?

Unfortunately, the tremor racing down my spine couldn't be entirely attributed to the grasp of a powerful opponent. And perhaps that's why my rebuttal came out with so much bite. "Oh, yes. The expert on sibling relations. Did you show your big brother to his room, sedate him with sleeping pills, then sneak out for a beer? Is that why you dared to leave his presence when the poor little pack leader might very well be stubbing his toe at this very instant?"

Only the slight twitch of Gunner's left eyebrow proved that my verbal attack had struck home. But he *did* release my wrists and take one small step backwards, the musk of predatory alpha thinning until I was finally able to think...

...and to remember that I had a friend here in the convenience store. Over the werewolf's shoulder, I caught the eye of a clerk I'd gone to high school with and shook my head briefly in response to his raised eyebrows. No, I didn't need help. Not against one annoying shifter whose worst fault was a tendency to show up in the wrong place at the wrong moment.

"A beer," Gunner answered, picking the least incendiary part of my tirade to fixate upon. "Good idea. How about I buy you a bottle and we can talk about why you purposefully lost tonight's match?"

His words followed me more closely than the whistled melody had as I slid away from his tantalizing body heat and stalked toward colder quarry. Bread—not the kind Kira liked the best but the cheaper sort she would still smile upon. Life was all about compromise and tonight's Arena windfall wouldn't last long if I fed her tween appetite with name-brand morsels.

"I didn't lose on purpose," I lied vaguely, trying to decide whether my kid sister was still on a 1% kick or whether we could return to the whole milk we'd both enjoyed until the previous autumn. Unfortunately, the girls in her grade were brutal on body fat, and Kira embraced their barbed comments even though our kind required far more calories than the average couch-potato twelve-year-old.

Better safe than sorry, I decided with a grimace. Plucking out a gallon of low-fat, I froze as Gunner's warm breath counteracted the cold emanating from the refrigerated case.

"Or we could change the subject," the werewolf murmured, voice so low the clerk had no chance of overhearing. "My brother and I are hunting something very specific. My gut says you're the key to finding it. We'd pay very well if you helped us track it down."

I was the key to finding whatever these brothers were looking for here in a city their pack had ignored for several decades?

A shiver far less enticing than the ones that had been impacting me previously ran down my spine. Slowly, unwillingly, I turned to meet Gunner's gaze. "What are you looking for?"

"Something," the werewolf answered unhelpfully before allowing silence to descend between the two of us. His face was as expressionless as a still pool of water, but I could smell his amusement that I'd risen to the bait.

Gritting my teeth, I tried to focus on lunch meat. Perhaps if I splurged on a hunk of salami my kid sister's eyes would light up at the treat like the noon-day sun....

But despite my best impulses to the contrary, Gunner's hook lodged itself in my gills and pulled me relentlessly out of the safely deep waters. What were these werewolves looking for? Did it have anything to do with Kira and my kind?

My inherent curiosity sent me leaning forward as I pondered, heart rate elevated more than it had been by my recent near miss. Still, I opened my mouth to give the smart answer, the correct answer. Because I shouldn't spend any more time than necessary around the new pack leader's brother. Kira and I couldn't afford to risk our skins just to enjoy salami on a weekly rather than a yearly basis...or to douse inquisitiveness that was so painfully inflamed.

But before I could come up with an appropriately scathing comment, a trickle of melody slid beneath the crack in the door. The same strangely familiar tune I'd heard while walking down the street....

And in response I paled, dropping Kira's bread on top of a display of candy bars as my fingers abruptly lost their hold on the potential purchase. My instinct had been right and my pursuer hadn't given up. Which presented an even worse situation than I'd previously been in. Because I was now standing beside an eagle-eyed werewolf, unable to use my inherent abilities to gnaw my way out of the trap before it could close around my leg.

I bit my lip as I began lowering the jug of milk to the floor in instinctive disburdenment. But the liquid would rot there if the clerk didn't notice in time to slide the jug back into the case. And upcoming evasive maneuvers would be less obvious if I hung onto one potential purchase at least.

So I clutched the cold handle, fingers digging into plastic as I spoke to the werewolf who'd delayed me—purposefully? accidentally?—long enough for the whistler to catch up. "Hold that thought," I told him, offering Kira's full-blast-sunshine smile and hoping the expression was as heart-stopping on me as it was on her. After all, I needed every advantage I could muster if I intended to slide out the 7-Eleven's window right under a werewolf's nose.

Then, without further explanation, I padded into the filthy bathroom, twirled the lock to solidify the barrier...and hoisted myself plus my purloined jug of milk through the tiny opening set too high in the wall for an average human to clamber in or out.

"I'll pay you back tomorrow," I whispered into the night air, knowing the clerk would understand the delay in cash flow. Still, the debt squeezed at my star ball, dragging at my footsteps as I beat a hasty retreat.

Chapter 6

"**O**of. Get off me!" I woke to fur in my face along with my sister's smug grin peering through the small gap between covers and red tail fluff.

Oh, and did I mention Kira was in fox form? I could feel the year's seventh tardy slip falling into my hands already.

"You need to shift and shower and eat and...did you finish your homework last night while I was fighting?"

The fox who was my sister leapt off my pillow a millisecond before my fingers would have closed around her snow-white belly. Soft feet landed on top of the tiny dorm-style refrigerator three feet away from my pull-out sofa-bed, and I decided to take that as a yes to the breakfast and a no to the shifting, showering, and homework. At least we'd get the bare necessities done today.

"Kira, I'm serious," I grumbled, even as I pulled out the wide cereal bowl that was easy for a snout to scoop food out of. Half a box of off-brand cheerios, a healthy glug of last night's stolen milk, and my sister was at least eating her breakfast...even if she was still perched on top of the fridge while doing so.

Of course, Kira was also a *fox*, so nothing came easily. Three bites later, my young charge lost interest in food and hummed a request instead, drawing our mother's star ball toward us out of the only bedroom our apartment boasted. The golden glow was the reason my sister was able to shift before coming of age, but it was also the last remnant of our dead mother's spirit. So I didn't argue as Kira leapt away from her half-finished meal and used the solidified magic as a platform, allowing her to dance across the room without touching the ground. Instead, I smiled fondly...then froze as I remembered the jolt of understanding that had run through my head as I succumbed to slumber the night before.

The whistle in the dark alley hadn't been just an eerily unfamiliar melody. Instead, it had matched the tinny sound made by our mother's nearly forgotten music box. Or so I thought. I'd need to rustle up long-packed-away possessions to be sure....

"I'm serious about that shower, Kira," I told my sister absently, turning away as my own star ball joined the circus without any explicit request to do so on my part. "And you know you have a test today in..." I racked my brain, gave up "...in *something*. So, please, at least bring the relevant book to school."

Kira *hadn't* done her homework and *had* forgotten her test—I could see the guilt in her beady eyes. But she was a fox who was snatching bites of a filling breakfast in between her capers, so she'd land—both literally and metaphorically—on her feet.

Confident that my sister was taken care of, I took the five steps to her bedroom in a rush. Clothes covered every available surface and it took longer than it should have to pick my way through to the rather empty closet. I'd need to find an hour this afternoon to tidy up just in case Social Services dropped by for a surprise inspection....

For now, though, I was more interested in the boxes on the closet's top shelf than in the clothes all over the floor. It had been so long since I'd been up there that dust bunnies gave even Kira's slovenly ways a run for their money.

And yet...the box I was looking for was swept as smooth as if it held a daily necessity. And when I pulled down the battered cardboard container, the item in my hands wasn't nearly as heavy as it should have been.

Inside, a few photos and childhood drawings fluttered against my fumbling fingers. But the music box, the jewelry, Mama's cherished possessions—every single one of them was gone without a trace.

"I'M SORRY," KIRA WHISPERED as her class poured into the gym for third-period PE. She'd clearly been working on this apology for the entirety of her first two classes, because the rest of it came out in a rush. "I should have talked to you first. But selling Mama's belongings was the only way I could think of to pay the water and electric bills. And it wasn't as if we were *using* any of that stuff."

"It's okay," I told my sister, even though it really wasn't. But I was disappointed in myself more than in Kira. Disappointed that my thirteen-years-younger sister had taken household expenses upon herself without me noticing...and, I'll admit it, disappointed that I'd never see our dead mother's possessions again. Just because Dad—and then I—had hidden the items away in a dusty box while avoiding all mention of our shadowed heritage didn't mean I was willing to sell the items on Ebay.

Still, my day brightened a little when Kira accepted my words at face value. She shot me a sunny smile before bouncing over to the opposite side of the room where three girls waited. And even though they were entirely human and dressed far better than I'd ever managed to deck out my ward, they still welcomed her into their midst with cheery greetings and sparkling eyes.

"Wanna see a magic trick?" my sister asked as she joined them, pulling out three scarves and a deck of cards before her companions could reply. And I'll admit it—I let the pre-class bustle linger longer than usual so Kira could enjoy her moment in the limelight. Gave everyone three long minutes to gab and gossip and make objects disappear.

But, finally, I could drag my heels no longer. "Line up in two rows. We're going to start with drills parrying four and six," I bellowed in a voice guaranteed to garner even argumentative sixth graders' attention.

The girls obeyed as sluggishly as Kira had caved to the necessity of her morning shower. But, eventually, clanging practice swords proved that nineteen over-indulged princesses—and my orphaned sister—would go to math class with hearts racing and endorphin levels elevated.

Which should have been good enough. But my skin itched and my eyes kept being drawn to the three students in front of and beside my kid sister. So I drifted closer to hear what kind of muttered secrets were being exchanged along with sword blows.

"Keep the tip of your blade pointed at your opponent's chest while you parry," I murmured to a rather over-excited redhead as I worked my way closer to the girls in question. "Hand parallel to the floor," I corrected another student, angling toward the girls upon whom the entirety of my attention now rested.

And then I could hear their chatter above the din...at which point I finally realized that Kira had been lying when she told me everything was just peachy at school. "Maybe you can use your *magic tricks* to get Jared's attention," Kira's current opponent sneered, eyeballing my sister's body in a way that made the shorter girl's cheeks flush crimson.

"Or maybe you could make *yourself* disappear. That'd be a good one." The girl on Kira's right was barely moving her sword while she indulged in a verbal offensive of her own.

"I don't know why they let gooks into our school," the third student interjected contemplatively. "Asian kids are supposed to be smart, but we can all tell from Kira's uniform that she's a scholarship student. She can't even pay her own way."

At which point, I stopped even pretending to pay attention to the rest of the class. Started sprinting toward my sister...even though I knew any intervention would come far too late.

Because Kira might have been abjectly apologetic at the beginning of class, but all foxes have a temper and Kira was no exception. Unlike me, however, she tended to save words for later and to dive straight into the physical when cornered and outmatched.

So I wasn't surprised when my nose caught the faintest hint of fur as Kira unleashed a tiny fraction of the vulpine agility she'd been holding back earlier in the session. I wasn't surprised when she knocked off each girl's face mask with a quick dip and jerk of her blunt-tipped sword. One, two, three helmets clanged onto the floor then one, two, three sets of manicured fingertips rose to feminine throats in unintentional unison.

Behind me, air pushed against my back as someone opened the door leading to the hallway. But I ignored whoever was coming or going, channeling all of my attention upon my sister as I turned my sprint into something a little faster. Because I'd learned the hard way that an angry Kira was unable to think through the consequences of her actions. And, like the rest of her family, my kid sister was remarkably good with a sword.

Sure enough, before I could interpose myself between the four battling students, my sister's practice blade rose for a fourth time. Thankfully, the swords I'd handed out to these children boasted unsharpened edges and a soft rubber ball protecting each tip. Still, any hunk of metal can do real damage if wielded by a pro.

Kira was well on her way to becoming such an expert.

"*Don't*!" I demanded, sending one curt word where my feet had failed to carry me.

But my sister's lashes didn't even flicker in response to my order. Instead, she slapped those bitchy girls with the flat of her blade so fast the first wasn't even crying before the third was being similarly assaulted. Within seconds, three red welts stood out against perfectly moisturized skin...then the floodgates opened up.

"I...I...I...." the leader of the posse stuttered, spinning to take in her damaged face in the mirror that covered one entire wall. "My face is ruuuiiiinnned!" another girl wailed. For her part, the third student was too overwhelmed to even emote verbally. Instead, she collapsed into a silent heap, cradling her injured cheek in both hands.

"Maybe you should grow up and shut up," Kira whispered in a voice blazing with passion. "Maybe you shouldn't talk about things you don't understand."

Meanwhile, behind me, an equally familiar tone cut through the room's hushed silence. "Mai, Kira, I'll see you both in my office immediately," the headmistress informed us. "Injured parties report to the nurse's station. And the rest of you, it's time to go to math."

Chapter 7

"I've been concerned for some time about the levels of violence in your classes," Ms. Underhill informed me as I sank into one of the two seats in front of her desk. The armchairs were obscenely comfortable...but they were also considerably lower to the floor than average. Given my already short stature, I felt like a child peering up at an adult from my present vantage point, precisely the effect the headmistress was going for.

"Fencing isn't about violence," Kira countered from the perch she'd taken on the edge of her seat, her chin level with the desk rather than hidden beneath it like mine was. "It's about control and restraint and..."

I could repeat our father's words just as glibly as my sister was currently doing, but something told me Ms. Underhill wasn't going to be impressed by the well-rehearsed refrain. Not when Kira had recently used her so-called control and restraint to mark the daughters of three major donors to the academy.

"We apologize," I said instead. "Kira was out of line and I should have been able to stop her." I swallowed, knowing the school had a zero-tolerance policy toward physical aggression. This wasn't my sister's first offense, so she would definitely be suspended. The question was—for how long? And when the suspension was over, would she be allowed to return to class?

As if sensing my distress, Kira rushed in to back me up as she always did. "Yes, I'm *so* sorry Ms. Underhill. I take complete responsibility for my actions. I'll apologize to Missy and Callie and Veronica too. I swear, nothing like this will *ever* happen again."

Her face was so open and candid, her tone so gushing. And the effect would have been believable too...if all three of us hadn't remembered the other incidents in vivid technicolor.

There was that time in the cafeteria when my sister had grown bored and started a food fight so severe the entire place had to be shut down for the rest of the afternoon for cleanup. The time she'd gotten tossed out of class after correcting her Latin teacher's pronunciation then reciting a very bawdy ballad in a language only she and he understood. And how could we forget the way my tiny sister had beaten up three over-sized football players who were trying to take advantage of a slip of a girl behind the bleachers?

Kira's heart was in the right place...but sometimes her brain didn't come along for the ride.

So my relief was palpable when the faintest hint of a smile pulled up the corners of Ms. Underhill's thin lips. "*You* will be spending one week thinking through your choices during an out-of-school suspension," the headmistress told my sister firmly before returning her attention to me.

"I appreciate your generosity." Only when my lungs expanded to their full extent for the first time in several minutes did I realize that oxygen hadn't been making its way to my lungs quite right ever since the headmistress's voice had shown up in my class at exactly the wrong moment. Kira needed structure in her life and someone other than me pushing her academically. She'd been bored out of her skull at the public school, and a bored Kira was like a grenade with the pin removed. Bystanders had better brace themselves and wait for the detonation.

The academy was our family's haz-mat suit. Being able to maintain that protection in light of Kira's recent actions was more than I'd dared to expect.

So I struggled up out of the depths of the armchair and met Ms. Underhill's eyes as best I could from two feet lower. Did she sit on a pillow back there to elevate her height? "I promise you that Kira will come back to school on her best behavior and ready to learn...."

"I'm sure she will be," the headmistress interjected. "But that's not the reason I brought you here today. As I mentioned earlier, I'm concerned that *swordplay* is an inappropriate activity for impressionable young minds. Control and restraint can be learned just as admirably at a gentler sport. Something like *ballet.*"

I cringed, imagining myself in a pink leotard barking orders at a roomful of tutu-clad kindergartners. But this was what I'd signed on for when I promised my dying father that I'd raise Kira myself rather than losing her to the foster-care system. So I merely nodded, keeping my clenched fists hidden beneath the overhang of the desk. "I understand," I agreed. "I can do that."

"No, I don't think you *do* understand," Ms. Underhill contradicted. Her head tilted, her mouth pursed, and for a split second I thought the old battle ax felt sorry for me. "I'm afraid I've found someone else to fill your position. Your final paycheck will go out in the mail tomorrow...along with a bill for the rest of Kira's tuition at the normal rate."

"I'LL BE BETTER OFF without that school anyway." Kira was back on top of the cemetery wall, but she wasn't dancing through our walk home this time around. Instead, she was skulking, shoulders hunched and feet kicking out at every pebble that dared stray into her path.

Her words, in contrast, remained perfectly controlled as she laid out a plan that would have made our father weep if he wasn't rotting in his grave. "At the public school, I can land an A without any effort. Which means I can get a job. We'll be a two-breadwinner family. We can buy a TV and a better sofa. We can eat salami. That's how it *should* be. Really, Mrs. Underhill is doing us a favor. I'll write her a thank-you note as soon as we get home."

Despite the evenness of Kira's monologue, she clearly lamented the lost opportunity as much as I did. Because rocks went spraying out in every direction beneath a particularly virulent kick, and this time I had to dodge to prevent being struck.

"How about a milkshake?" I countered. "Or a candy bar? We can talk about school later."

After all, I'd learned the hard way that it was a recipe for failure trying to out-argue my sister once she'd dug her heels in. Kira *was* going back to the academy, but I wouldn't press the issue until I figured out how to pay the full-price tuition. Until then, I might as well keep us both calm so our fox natures didn't make us say things we'd later regret.

Kira, on the other hand, had no such compunction about speaking before thinking. "*You* said I needed to steer clear of sugar. *You* said it made me volatile."

I had to laugh at my sister's rebuttal...because, really, how much more volatile could Kira get after being kicked out of school for bitch-slapping three classmates? "I think just this once you can handle a sugar high," I started...

...then yelped as hard hands grabbed onto my shoulders while the sidewalk spun away from beneath my feet. There were male figures all around me now, the emergence of lanky legs and leering faces proving that I'd been too focused upon my sister's hurt feelings and not focused enough upon potential dangers impinging from the outside world.

But Kira was perched on top of a wall in a place of momentary safety. "*Run!*" I told her seconds before a hand landed atop my open mouth, strangling all further sound.

The teenager's palm tasted like grease and salt, and I was 99% certain my opponent hadn't washed after using the restroom. *Gross.* Still, the eyes that advanced toward me were entirely human. And the male's scent was more fast-food pickles than incipient fur.

So I didn't bother dulling my reflexes. Just hooked my knees around Pickle Breath's ankles and *pulled* so hard he hit the ground with an audible thud even as I struggled to regain my own footing.

Which didn't leave me in the clear, of course. Not with four other gang members still reaching toward me, their hands making up in number what they lacked in supernatural speed.

Despite the advancing front of heady testosterone, I stole a moment to peer at my sister as she perched atop the wall just where I'd left her. Predictably, Kira had completely ignored my previous commandment. If I didn't miss my guess, she was currently trying to decide which gang member to leap upon first.

"Go home," I mouthed again, hoping our opponents had forgotten about the girl's presence. Just imagining what would happen if they grabbed my innocent sister sent my chest shrinking in on itself, forcing life-giving air out of my lungs....

So I let the barest hint of fox fill my features as I glared directly at her. Let Kira know from my sharpening teeth and darkening eyes that I was serious about being obeyed this time around.

And, to my relief, Kira hesitated only one more second before nodding. Then she spun on her heel and sprinted away so quickly none of the gang members would have been able to catch her even if they'd tried.

The distant shriek of a city bus's air brakes promised Kira would be safe within seconds if she played her cards right. Which left me with no one to worry about except my lonesome.

Good thing I had aggressions to work out of my own system since the field was currently rather overbalanced on my opponents' behalf.

Chapter 8

F ive against one was a bit much even for me, but I didn't bother turning my star ball into a sword this time around. Not when goons like the ones before me measured the world in terms of greater and lesser forces. If I whipped a blade out of nowhere and vanquished them today, they'd just try again with weapons of their own tomorrow. On the other hand, if I beat up five bozos using nothing except my own body...well, maybe they'd leave my kid sister alone should she ever sneak out and walk down this street by herself in the future.

So I dipped beneath the closest male's grasping arms and used his own momentum to push him toward the pavement. Thug two received a kick to the chest and three didn't see the arm-twist coming. Which left only the tallest gang member standing...plus Pickle Breath, who was clambering back to his feet on my right-hand side.

The recent show of strength really should have been enough to dull their aggressions. After all, these teenagers were just kids barely older than my sister. So I gave them an opportunity to cut their losses without further bruising doled out by me.

"I recommend you walk away while you still can," I told the tall guy who apparently believed in leading from the rear. Then, glancing at the three teens still catching their breath atop the pavement, I added, "Or crawl. Whichever works best for you."

"You need to pay up if you want protection in our neighborhood," Tall Guy countered, acting as if he had a full posse behind him rather than being the only member of his gang with all body parts still intact. "We've carried your ass long enough. Stay and pay, or go and..."

I couldn't decide whether or not to roll my eyes as Tall Guy struggled to come up with a word that rhymed with "go." Because I'd felt bad about beating up gang members who were really just confused teenagers. But if their leader was going to force the issue...well, I hadn't enjoyed a good fight in over a week due to Ma Scrubbs' requirement that I lose my most recent Arena match.

"Go and owe?" I suggested, taking a single step forward. Now that I thought about it, I couldn't really blame Kira for beating up those girls earlier in the day. Not when my own feet were itching with the urge to leap and kick, not when my fingers tingled with the knowledge that battle was imminent....

"Let the water flow," my dead mother's voice warned me. And her words materializing in my brain shocked me just as much the second time around as they had the first.

Perhaps that's why I merely stood there as a faint scent of musky fur washed over me. Since when did werewolves follow me around day after day? And did my maternal ghost's sudden chattiness have anything to do with the presence of a shifter where one didn't belong?

Unfortunately, Tall Guy took advantage of my surprise to get the jump on me. The teenager wasn't willing to be laughed at in front of his comrades, and he was apparently willing to do something about that affront. I barely caught a flicker of movement before he was reaching into the back of his baggy trousers and pulling out a revolver that changed the odds in an instant.

The weapon reflected a beam of pure sunlight into my retinas before tilting so I stared down the dark barrel instead. "Die, ho," the gang leader said grimly.

Then he pulled the trigger.

WITH A WEREWOLF NEARBY, I couldn't dodge out of the way of the oncoming bullet. But I *could* use my star ball to protect myself.

Apparently it was too much to ask to manipulate magic into a solid barrier while also bracing myself against the impact though. Because the cartridge hit dead center in my chest so hard it sent me sprawling, the scab on my hand scraping loose against the pavement as I attempted to catch myself before my skull hit the ground.

And even though I didn't crack my head open, I *did* land with enough force that I ended up unable to do more than watch as the newcomer launched himself onto those poor thugs with the full force of a pissed-off werewolf. My protector was outwardly human but inwardly bestial. And once I finally blinked tears out of my eyes sufficiently to make out my ally's identity, I found myself unsurprised by the realization that I was far too familiar with this ravening beast.

A swordsman's grace in an athlete's body. Gunner. Of course. Who else would be tailing me so slyly that he could come to my supposed rescue at just the wrong moment...yet again?

The werewolf-in-human-clothing wasn't even breathing heavily when he paused thirty seconds later to assess the damage. His opponents, on the other hand, were another matter entirely. Tall Guy whined like a nap-deprived toddler, his arm broken and his pistol kicked twenty yards away. Pickle Breath swore steadily, but even he kept his eyes down and his head bowed in instinctive submission to the beast within their midst.

And the other three kids? They'd run off the moment Gunner turned his attention elsewhere, proving they were smarter than their so-called boss.

"Mai is under my protection," Gunner growled then, words barely human as he knelt atop Tall Guy's prone figure with the teen's unbroken arm twisted up behind his back. The werewolf's muscles rippled with his attempt to maintain humanity, and his dark eyebrows lowered into a glowering frown. "You so much as look at her funny, and your future ends precipitously. Do you understand what I'm saying here?"

I wasn't so sure Tall Guy knew the meaning of the word "precipitously," but he certainly got the gist of the werewolf's threat anyway. Because the boy cringed in on himself so severely he appeared shorter than I was. And his breathing became so sporadic he managed no more than a frantic nod as I took advantage of the lull to pry myself off the pavement and pad over to their side.

Not that I wanted to put myself between an angry alpha and his quarry. But while Gunner might have seemed like a nice-enough guy in the Arena, I didn't trust any werewolf to protect the innocent. And Tall Guy—despite his chosen profession—was innocent enough.

So I twisted half of my star ball into the shape of a dagger, secreting the weapon beneath my sleeve where it would be accessible if Gunner turned overly aggressive once I moved to interrupt. Then I opened my mouth and accepted the werewolf's annoying yet helpful support. "And my sister as well," I murmured just loudly enough for the shifter to hear me without impinging upon Tall Guy's attempts to smooth his gasps into words.

"And Mai's sister," Gunner added, driving his knee deeper into Tall Guy's kidneys while twisting the poor kid's arm up higher into the air. "The sister is mine also. *Swear it.*"

The scent of fur grew stronger as Gunner's humanity continued slipping. And I'd already opened my mouth to let the kid off the hook when Tall Guy finally forced out a babbling plea for mercy. "Yes, yes, yes, *yes!*" the teenager shrieked, writhing within the larger male's grip.

At which point I placed one hand on Gunner's shoulder to remind him that my former opponents were only human. If he broke them, they'd remain broke.

Alpha werewolves hate being contradicted, but Gunner's response was more extreme than I'd anticipated. Because before I could so much as skitter sideways, his hand reached out to grab my wrist with the speed of a striking cobra. Then his nostrils flared as he took in the liquid pooling across my palm.

"Blood," he noted. At which point his gaze landed on the hole in my sweatshirt and his eyes widened. "You've been shot."

Chapter 9

Gunner rose to his feet so abruptly I would have lost my balance if his hands hadn't been tearing at the neckline of my sweatshirt, attempting to rip fabric away from my skin. Out of the corner of one eye, I caught sight of the remaining gang members fleeing the scene of their defeat. But I wasn't concerned about teenage hoodlums any longer. Instead, I was fighting off a male who outweighed me by approximately a ton of muscle and who possessed supernatural speed and agility to boot.

"Stop!" I demanded, bringing one knee up to hit the male equivalent of an eject button. Because, yes, I'll admit it—I had previously found the alpha werewolf as enticing and dangerous as a shiny new rapier. But I didn't intend to assuage my curiosity on an open city street.

Unfortunately, Gunner's instincts proved far too well-honed to fall prey to the typical female self-defense moves. Instead, the alpha's easy twist out of my reach suggested that he was as adept at street fighting as he was at protecting his brother. And this time around, my throat tightened as I realized I was trapped within the vise-grip of werewolf arms.

Well, not quite trapped. The icy dagger slid down into my left fingers with facility despite the mandates of gravity begging it to move in the opposite direction. And my lips twitched into

45

a smirk as I recalled how easily a lefty strike typically worked its way through an opponents' unwitting guard.

But before I could decide between the long-lasting damage of a stab and the shock value of a swipe, the fabric of my shirt tore at last with a resounding *riiiiiip*. Then cold air rushed across my chest at the same moment Gunner flipped the dagger out of my hand with an almost-gentle bend of his wrist.

I was both disarmed and in dishabille. And while either state might have been enough to leave me shaken, it was the separation from my star ball that struck like a punch to my gut. The fragment of my soul soared away before I could beg it to change trajectory, and I bent inward as my strength fled right along with my blade.

"I need to see where you're *wounded*," Gunner growled, his words laden with more emotion than seemed justified by the ugly gray of my sports bra. Oh, right, the bullet hole. I shook my head woozily, trying to recall why showing the handsy alpha my holeless skin wasn't the obvious route out of this untenable situation.

And as I pondered, Gunner took matters into his own hands. "Easy does it," he murmured, voice hoarse with emotion. One huge hand slid down to press almost gently against my lower back while the other leveraged my shoulders up. Then chilly air gaped down the dramatically enlarged neckline of my sweatshirt, bringing my barely covered chest closer to the werewolf's searching eyes.

IT WAS HARD TO THINK with a third of my soul glinting against the pavement two body lengths away. So despite the sure knowledge that retrieving the star ball via magic was a bad idea, I nudged at the pseudo-metal with my mind's eye, dragging it inch by inch across the road as stealthily as an alley cat stalked a mouse.

And the mere change in direction of my soul fragment snapped the rest of my brain back into focus. *He can't know what I am,* I realized, hoping it wasn't already too late.

Luckily, I could work quickly when haste was necessary. Calling upon the rest of my magic with far less ceremony than usual, I molded the icy star-ball fragment into a medallion. Sent out a tendril of magic to solidify into a gold chain looped around my neck. Then mental fingers slipped the bulky disc into my left bra cup a split second before Gunner's hand-on-shoulders momentum bared my unclothed chest to view.

It turned out I needn't have hurried though. Because the werewolf who had been so aggressive one moment earlier paused before digging into my underwear. His fingers hovered atop the second layer of fabric while his scent grew subtly more human as he overcame the instincts of his beast.

"I need to look at...." He paused, averted his eyes, and didn't quite manage to complete the thought as the faintest tinge of red infused his cheeks.

The abrupt shyness from a formerly brash alpha was endearing. So rather than snapping back in retaliation for earlier abuses, I merely pulled the medallion out of its hiding place with a jerk to the chain that hadn't existed seconds before. "The bullet never hit me," I informed him, speaking as slowly as I did with the most annoying of my sixth graders. "It's the old Bible-in-the-breast-pocket routine. No wound. No blood. No reason for you to be pawing at my breasts."

Seconds after I spoke, though, I realized the error in my logic. Kira would have rolled her eyes at such an obvious continuity flaw in someone else's magic trick. Because if the medallion had been inside my bra cup from the get-go...why was there no hole in that second layer of fabric? Why wasn't there the bulge of a bullet breaking up the gentle curve of my breast?

Moving as swiftly as I could, I pulled a safety pin out of nowhere...or, rather, out of the back of the medallion, which shrank by half a centimeter as it lost a twentieth of its mass. Then I covered up the evidence quite literally, pinning my sweatshirt back together with hands that trembled only slightly.

Meanwhile, the boomeranged dagger nudged at my boot, its peregrinations complete. Just what I needed—to draw further attention to inconsistencies in my spur-of-the-moment solution. Still, I couldn't just leave it there.

So, neck prickling with danger, I bent down to collect the errant weapon, feeling absurd as I went through the motions of stashing a trickle of magic away in an imaginary sheath up one sleeve.

Up my *right* sleeve. Shit. Could I be more disingenuous?

Before me, the werewolf's brows furrowed in consideration. He knew something was cockeyed...which meant it was past time to make my escape.

"Thanks for nothing," I said grimly, turning away from a predator who possessed the means, motive, and opportunity to snap my neck between his long fingers. Then, forcing my feet not to break into a run, I headed blindly toward the far end of the block.

Chapter 10

Unfortunately, I'd only taken a single step when Gunner's hand came down upon my shoulder. And I hated myself for the tingle of awareness that had nothing to do with the werewolf tendency to hunt fox shifters as one of his fingers slid sideways to brush up against my bare skin.

"Wait," Gunner ordered. Or rather...requested? Because there was no electric tingle of alpha compulsion seasoning the single syllable this time. He wasn't telling. He was asking...well, as much as an alpha could bring himself to ask.

I was too much of a teacher not to reward good behavior. So I swiveled back to face him, arching an eyebrow even as I cocked my head. "What?"

"I wanted you to know the offer's still open." Confusion must have painted itself across my face because Gunner elaborated. "The job. My brother headed back to headquarters this morning, but I'm here for the duration. Well, not literally *here*. In town." He stopped himself before explanation turned into babble, held out what appeared to be a newly printed business card.

Curiosity forced me to accept the small rectangle of card stock. The werewolf had rented an office in the city while searching for a single Something? From the address, the space couldn't have come cheap.

"I'm not going to take a job I know nothing about," I countered, even as dollar signs danced through my head like moonbeams. How much, I wondered, might the werewolf in front of me spend hiring a local guide and investigative assistant? Enough to pay Kira's tuition? Enough to buy my voracious sibling salami every day of the week?

"I wouldn't ask you to do anything nefarious," the werewolf in front of me promised. His eyes were hooded, his voice sweet as honey. "There's something dangerous walking these streets and I intend to find it. To keep people like your sister safe. There are elements involved I think you might be familiar with...."

Only when his words trailed off did I realize that I'd been inching closer with each of his syllables, my chin tilting upward as if Gunner was a magnet and I was iron filings drawn toward him through no action of my own. *Bad idea, Mai*, I berated myself. Forcing myself to take one long step backward, I decided then and there that Kira and I would be better off living on ramen noodles rather than placing ourselves in the sight line of a seductively smooth alpha like this one.

Unfortunately, the star chain around my neck was unimpressed by my decision to be my own master. Instead, the mere thought of food was enough to remind it of last night's unpaid milk money, and now the magic sent cold trickles shivering over my shoulders and turning icier by the second. I *needed* to get to that 7-Eleven sooner rather than later. I *needed* to pay off my debt....

"Thanks but no thanks," I told the waiting werewolf, tucking his business card into one pocket while turning back in the direction from which I'd come. I'd hand over three bucks for the milk, then my star-ball-turned-conscience would leave me alone.

And even though my life was tricky enough without werewolves in it, I was subtly disappointed when Gunner's footsteps failed to follow me down the block. Apparently, though, lack of sound didn't equate to lack of movement. Because werewolf breath soon warmed the back of my neck despite the distance I'd moved since his last words.

"You can go straight home," the werewolf noted, apparently having realized why I'd switched directions without me having to explain the action in words. "I paid for your milk."

This time, the lizard of debt inside my chest cavity scrambled up my spine with scratchy claws even as Mama warned inside my brain: *Specks of dust slowly accumulate into mountain ranges.*

"Let me pay you back," I started, knowing my mother was right. I couldn't afford to be indebted to a werewolf....

But this time Gunner was the one backing away, was refusing the bills I fumbled out toward him in an effort to stave off further star-ball compulsions. "It was my pleasure," my companion answered, the distance between us growing with every word. "Maybe next time you'll let me buy you a beer. Or at least we could drink some milk together. You have my card."

He was flirting. Sweetly almost. If only he wasn't a werewolf, perhaps I would have said yes.

Instead, I squashed the niggle of complaint from my star ball, shook my head once, then swiveled around yet again to head in my original direction. If the werewolf didn't want my money, then I'd save it for my sister. It was time to get home and check on Kira.

I SHOULD HAVE BEEN relieved to finally achieve the anteroom of my den, but I winced as I pushed open the heavy fire door that separated stairwell from hallway. Because my least favorite person was waiting on the faded welcome mat outside our apartment, and I really could have done without dealing with Simon tonight.

"Mai," the gangly social worker greeted me, his voice as droopy as the wrinkles around his eyes. "I've been waiting for twenty minutes."

"Shi—oot," I parried. "So sorry about that."

Meanwhile, my mind was running a mile a minute. What was Simon doing here? Had he found out about my lost job and about Kira's precarious school situation? Was he ready to live up to past insinuations that my sister would be better off placed in another home?

If our conversation had been a cage fight, I would have been backpedaling rapidly while hoping my hind end didn't end up against the chain-link before I came up with a strategy other than retreat. Luckily, Simon took pity on my confusion before I let anything particularly incriminating slip. "Did you forget we had a home visit planned for today?"

A home visit? That's all this was? "Yeah," I admitted, brushing past the state employee as I turned my key in the lock. I'd likely noted down the date in my planner, then lost the reminder during Kira's ill-fated magic trick last week. After a building evacuation, two hours of mopping up sprinkler water, and a furious tirade by the apartment supervisor, the fate of my planner—and the dates of any upcoming home visits—had been the least of my concern.

As if reading my mind, Kira's bushy tail flicking apologetically from her perch atop the bedroom lintel and I found myself smiling instead of fuming. At least my sister had made it home safe and sound.

"So," Simon said, walking in behind me without invitation and settling into one of our two dining chairs. "How is everything going here?"

As he spoke, his gaze flicked around the tiny apartment, and I scurried along in its wake, moving dirty cereal bowls into the sink and picking up place mats that had been knocked onto the floor by fox action. It wasn't as if we lived in a pig sty, but I worked two jobs and Kira was a shifter cooped up in a one-bedroom apartment. Our home wasn't exactly spic and span.

On the other hand, I loved my sister, I neither used nor dealt drugs, and I didn't bring home pervert boyfriends who snuck into her room to fondle Kira's underage body while she slept. It was hard to believe this was the worst fostering situation Simon came in contact with. So I mustered a smile and offered foodstuffs I didn't actually have on hand rather than remarking upon the financial upset threatening Kira's and my lives. "Would you like some tea? Or a cookie?"

"No." Simon's mouth pursed as if the mere idea of eating something inside my home gave him the willies. He paused, then added: "Thank you."

We stared at each other in silence for enough seconds that the meeting began to feel profoundly awkward. Then the social worker pinned me down with a specific question I didn't know how to sidestep. "What is it you're working so hard not to tell me?"

The man was too astute for my own good. And I couldn't risk being caught up in an untruth.

So I went ahead and spilled the beans. "I lost my job at the school," I admitted. Then, figuring a little white lie wouldn't kill me, I added: "I've got several leads on new ones though. I swear to you, Kira isn't going to end up starving or on the streets. I just need a little time to work things out."

Rather than answering immediately, the social worker clambered back to his feet so he could take my hand. His palm was faintly damp and chilly, but I forced myself not to jerk away from the contact. Instead, I met Simon's gaze head on as he spoke in what he probably thought was a compassionate manner.

"I'll return Monday with my supervisor," he told me. "Please have Kira packed and ready. If your work situation hasn't improved dramatically by that point, I'm afraid we'll need to move your sister to a more appropriate home."

Chapter 11

"Stay here," I ordered Kira fifteen minutes later while molding my star ball into its favorite shape—a long, slender sword hanging at my hip where it would be easily accessible. "Don't go out, don't open the door, and don't let anybody in."

As I spoke, I kicked off my PE teacher shoes, donning high leather boots instead. Off went the fitted gym pants, on went the knife-resistant leather. A school-themed hoodie electrified my hair as it slid off my slender frame, then I drew my favorite shiny, black jacket back up around my shoulders like a shield.

"Go over the next chapter in your math book," I continued. "Just because you're suspended doesn't mean you can afford falling behind."

"Where are you going?" Kira spoke as she shifted, a shimmer of light and air turning fox into girl with the effortlessness of magic. She hadn't bothered leaping down from the lintel before transforming, so she ended up chinning herself onto the floor, landing as silently as she would have in her animal form.

Unfortunately, my sibling was even more inquisitive on two feet than she had been on four. And no more interested in schoolwork either.

"Tonight's not an Arena night," Kira pointed out, padding in a circle around me as she completely ignored all preceding instructions. Her agile fingers twitched my hair out from under the collar of my jacket and straightened my sword in its sheathe even as her equally clever tongue pinned me down verbally as only a little sister could. "Where else can we get enough money to satisfy Simon?"

I wasn't in the habit of lying to my sister, so I told her the cold, hard true. "From werewolves," I answered, eyes closing as I made a decision I knew in my heart would lead to yet more trouble. But I couldn't lose Kira to the foster-care system. And Gunner possessed both the funds and the ability to make my upcoming employment appear legitimate enough to satisfy even our dour social worker's unattainable standards.

I'd just have to keep a tight rein on my abilities until Gunner left town. Easy enough.

As if she was reading my mind, my sister raised herself on tiptoe until she could look me in the eye. Then she parroted back words I'd tossed in her direction far too often over the years. "Foxes and wolves don't mix. You can't let them know what we are."

My chest expanded with pride as I gazed upon a young woman growing into wisdom by the moment. "I won't," I started. But Kira wasn't done with her efforts to rule the roost.

"You need backup. I'm coming with you," she decided, dropping butt-to-linoleum by the door while yanking on recently discarded tennis shoes. The math textbook beside her was nudged subtly aside as she dressed, a sprawl of notebooks turning dog-eared and rumpled as she used them to pry dirt out from between her cleats. "I can be a distraction."

She sure could. Right now, for instance, I was distracted with worry that Dad might think my sister was better off in a wealthier household than the one I was able to pay for, or in a family where textbooks weren't used as doorstops. After all, our father had believed in education just as firmly as he believed in kinship. What would he think if I was forced to yank Kira out of the academy just because I couldn't come up with enough cash to pay the bill?

"No, you're not coming with me," I countered, squashing second thoughts even as I pulled up Gunner's address on my cell phone. The closest bus stop was a mile from the alpha's office and I'd have to make two changes to even get that far. "Math is an essential life skill," I muttered both to myself and to my sister. For example, math told me I couldn't afford a taxi...which meant I'd take the bus for the first leg then walk the rest.

I should have realized that Kira's mercurial nature was shifting from helpful to fretful, but I was too busy plotting out my plan of attack to notice the symptoms. Now, though, the leggy tween eased between my phone and my face, forcing me to pay attention to her expression. And I winced as I caught the red flush of anger brightening her cheeks.

"Kira..." I started.

"I'm not a *child*," my sister countered. "I deserve to be involved. I deserve to know what I *am*."

"We're foxes..."

Kira didn't even wait for me to finish that particular sentence. Instead, she pressed closer into my personal space, standing on tiptoes not so much in solidarity this time around as in an attempt to intimidate. "We're fox *shifters*," she corrected as if she was the adult and I was the child. "But what does that even mean? Why do the werewolves hate us if we're just like them except with red fur and better style? It doesn't make any sense."

She was right, unfortunately. But Mama had been my only link to knowledge about our heritage and our mother was long gone...or was she?

Absurdly, I waited ten long seconds for a voice in my head to illuminate the darkness. And during that delay, my sister's stewing erupted into outright rage. "If you don't want to tell me..." she started.

"I don't *know*, okay?" I snapped back, ashamed of myself even as I lost my temper. "Do you think turning into a parent at age eighteen came with a handbook? It *didn't*. I'm doing the best I can and you're not helping matters. Now do your homework then go to bed."

And, predictably, Kira lashed right back with her own fox fury. "I hate you," my usually sunny sister emoted, family cohesiveness and math textbooks forgotten in the face of my badly chosen honesty. Then the girl fled to her bedroom without another word and slammed the door behind her back.

Chapter 12

I'd managed to make the switch onto the blue line and was relaxing as the third city bus of the evening wended its way into the good part of town before it occurred to me that I wasn't the only person in the vehicle's shadowy posterior. How had I missed that hint of fur beneath the stench of unwashed bodies and spilled soda pop when I boarded ten minutes earlier? My only defense—that I had more important matters on my mind than getting jumped by a stray werewolf—failed to hold water when my attempt to swivel in search of further information was stilled by a flash of silver flicking in front of my eyes one millisecond before cold steel came to settle beneath my chin.

"Eh, eh, eh. Not so fast."

I froze, running through possibilities in my mind. Was this an unaffiliated drifter, an Atwood underling, or one of Jackal's henchmen? My opponent's identity should have made a difference, but the male's subsequent words turned off my rational side and prompted me to throw caution to the winds. "Your sister...." the male started.

And without giving him time to spit out whatever thinly veiled threat he'd dreamed up, I acted. One hand rose to pry his blade-holding fingers back into a painful reverse stretch even as my other arm leveraged me off the seat sufficiently to get my feet underneath my butt.

Then I was the one attacking. My sword was less than useless in such a confined situation, but I could spring upwards holding onto my opponent's hand while leaping. No wonder his knife clattered to the floor between us even as the male—scruffy, badly dressed, older than I'd expected—exploded into the aisle with teeth sharpening within his still-human mouth.

"You little bitch," he started, shaking out his right hand even as his left inched toward what appeared to be another knife marring the drape of his Hawaiian shirt. And here Kira thought *my* clothing needed assistance....

Wardrobe aside, I refused to be intimidated by my opponent's bulk or by his small-space-appropriate weapons. Instead, I bought a little breathing room with a verbal attack. "Nice flowers," I started. "But I thought Casual Friday wasn't until tomorrow...."

Before I could finish, I was sliding sideways, the non-slip matting beneath my feet insufficient to hold me in place as the bus driver slammed on his brakes. My stomach hit the plastic of the nearest seat back, breath whooshing out of me even as I scrabbled against the floorboards in search of my opponent's dropped weapon.

But the male was no longer attacking. Was, I realized as I looked up, instead halfway down the aisle where he'd been slung by the vehicle's abrupt halt.

Which meant his second knife was now poised half an inch away from the eyeball of a boy too young to be out by himself after dark. Yes, *I* was now safe from the werewolf's weaponry. But based on the curl of the shifter's upper lip, he was well aware that harm to an innocent was just as damaging as harm to myself.

The boy whimpered as the scent of smug shifter filled the enclosed space so densely it choked my attempted inhale. "The brain is right behind the eyeball," my werewolf opponent observed smoothly. "I learned that from a Hawaiian medicine woman. Are you ready to deal yet?"

THE BASTARD THOUGHT he had me over a barrel. But he'd missed my fingers closing around the knife recently abandoned on the bus's floor, and he must have also missed the memo that street fighters never back down.

So, unlike him, I attacked without warning. Didn't open my mouth or even flick my eyes to give away my intentions. Just twisted and flung the knife in one unerring movement, gaze following the blade as it sliced through my opponent's sleeve and bicep, ripping him away from his current victim and pinning the male against the back of the seat in front of them both.

The werewolf howled in agony, the boy shrieked in terror...and I was slung around hard as handcuffs pinched shut around my left wrist. "Police! Don't move!" a human shouted in my ear. Then my face was squished up against a seat back while my right hand was wrenched up behind me, only the faint musk of receding werewolf suggesting what I'd see once I was finally allowed to stand erect.

My opponent had taken advantage of the tussle to flee, I noted. And the humans, predictably, took one look at my ragged clothing combined with the massive sword still belted at my waist and rewrote the past with chilling inaccuracy.

"She was attacking that boy!" a cane-wielding matron exclaimed, pointing at the child who'd survived the scuffle without a single scratch...thanks to me.

"She pulled a knife," the bus driver confirmed, watching as I was frog-marched down the aisle and out the front door of the bus. I'd nearly made it to my destination, I realized. Was standing in a residential neighborhood full of mansions and bigger mansions and vast expanses of emerald green grass.

And...werewolves. Because the scruffy male was long gone, but another shifter waited at the bottom of the bus steps. This one reminded me of a more wiry version of Gunner and Ransom with a wardrobe even Kira would have considered both stylish and smart. Another brother? A cousin? I couldn't be certain. Whatever his lineage, the mild-mannered shifter in his bespoke business suit was a good fit for talking the policeman off my back.

"Is there a problem, officer?" the not-quite-stranger asked, the query so clichéd it might as well have rolled off the lips of a B-rate movie actor. And yet, he managed to pull off the impression. Could almost have been readjusting a monocle as he superciliously stared the policeman down.

"This woman attacked a boy on a city bus..." the officer started. But the stranger cut him off with a single raised hand.

"Did you see the altercation in person? Was anyone injured?"

"Well, no...."

"Then I highly doubt you have your facts straight. Because this young woman is my house guest. Not a troublemaker in the least...although she *could* use a better tailor. I'll admit that part."

Together, the werewolf and the police officer looked me up and down, lips similarly pursed as they passed judgment on my thrift-store attire. Hey, it was better than a hot pink Hawaiian shirt....

And even though my escape from potential incarceration shouldn't have been that easy, the bus of witnesses was already rolling away down the street. Meanwhile, the officer before us apparently had no incentive to argue with a well-heeled resident of a top-tier neighborhood. "I apologize for any inconvenience," the official told me after a single second of consideration. Then air flowed in to replace the pinch of handcuffs, my former captor strolling away down the sidewalk before my rescuer could lodge an official complaint.

Which left me in the custody of a werewolf who had every reason to berate me at length for nearly revealing myself to humans. But the stranger just raised one eyebrow and shook his head slowly instead. "Not smart," he chided almost gently before adding: "Go home."

Then he left me there. Didn't ask what I was doing in his neighborhood or why I'd let myself fall into the hands of a human authority while looking only moderately human. Instead, the male swiveled away from me—who turns their back on an angry sword-woman?—then continued on his trajectory alone.

For half a second, I just stood there, shocked by the male's rudeness. But then I scurried after him, jogging slowly enough to appear human while following the shifter up the steps to the mansion that bore Gunner's address. I fully expected the male's chivalrous instincts to prompt him to wait for me at the entrance of the building, but instead the door literally clanged shut in my face.

Rubbing my bruised forehead with one hand, I reached out to turn the knob with the other. Only to find the barrier locked and unwilling to budge. Really? Nameless Dude was just going to retreat inside and shut me out behind him?

Which is when my fox nature took over entirely. Not bothering with the bell, I pounded on the wooden door with both fists. "Let me in!" I demanded, temper firing hotter with every blow.

"Just like a werewolf," I growled under my breath, so intent upon fuming and noisemaking that I didn't hear footsteps responding to my barrage of knocks. My hand was drawn back in preparation for further pounding when the door jerked open before me.

And that's how I came to punch an alpha werewolf in the nose.

Chapter 13

There was blood. And the scent of fur. And the wildest flash of rage in a broad-shouldered shifter's eyes.

Then I was being drawn inside, the door closing behind us, as Gunner grabbed a doily off a sideboard and held it up to his streaming nostrils. "You certainly know how to make an entrance," he said grimly, walking away from me just as quickly as his brother—cousin?—had.

Like the thinner werewolf I'd followed up the front steps, the one currently in front of me didn't bother glancing back to see if I followed as he sped through a series of rooms full of ebony furniture and Turkish rugs. Instead, he bellowed loudly enough for humans to hear from the sidewalk, calling out names of pack mates who came sprinting toward us from nooks and crannies I didn't have time to fully peruse as we rushed past.

"Liam," Gunner greeted my former savior as we reached a broad stairwell in the heart of the mansion. The alpha's voice was muffled by the table runner he'd snatched to replace the doily as he stopped barking out names and moved on to demands. "What else do we know?"

I wasn't sure how the dark-haired shifter had found time to reach the second story in the few short seconds I'd spent pounding on the door out front. But now Liam descended the stairs in a measured manner while answering the shifter who clearly outranked him by at least a bit. "We don't know much," Gunner's relative said, falling in beside his superior while subtly boxing me further away from the center of power. "And are you sure you want to talk in front of a ragamuffin off the streets?"

Ragamuffin? Did the male think he was living in Victorian-era England? And did that mean my potential job hadn't been okayed by the rest of the pack?

Gunner glanced at me for a split second only, his eyes piercing as he dropped the table runner to the floor and accepted the handkerchief another pack mate was thrusting into his hand. "Tell me," he ordered Liam without bothering to respond to the dig about my part in...whatever this was.

And this time, information was finally forthcoming. "The body was found in an alley," Liam offered, which snagged my attention in a way Gunner's vague job offers had not. A body didn't sound good. A body meant there was more going on than an overbearing alpha and my need to pay the bills.

"Unscented like the last one?" my maybe-boss queried.

Liam merely nodded by way of reply, leaving me to wonder if my understanding of the world was perhaps a smidge small-minded and naive. Because as best I could tell, everything in our world had a scent. After all, superior nostrils were half of my edge over human opponents in the Arena.

But I didn't have time to further ponder the issue, because Gunner was pushing through the back door and leading us all onto what appeared to be an industrial loading dock. "Address?" he queried as I took in the view.

There were two moving vans backed up to the elevated concrete porch, as if these shifters had settled into my home town for the duration rather than merely passing through on their way to greener pastures. In addition, a fleet of cars and SUVs promised the pack would have no problem getting around while they were in residence. Must be nice having so many wheels at your beck and call.

And, apparently, a driver. Because Liam angled ahead of his relative at last, opening the driver's side door of the closest SUV. "I'll take you there."

The move appeared properly obsequious. However, for the first time, Gunner slowed the pack's forward momentum as his hand closed upon the reedier male's forearm. "No," the alpha said quietly...but not quietly enough to keep any of the nearby shifter ears from picking up on the mild rebuke. "Ransom would be lost without his personal secretary. He expects you home tonight. Stick to the plan."

THE WORDS WEREN'T COMMANDING, nor were they overtly revealing. Yet I read volumes of information streaming between the two males as they locked identical sienna eyes. Both shifters were looking out for their relative. Both understood that Ransom possessed some weakness requiring a trusted advisor present at all times.

Or that's the way Gunner saw the matter. Liam, it seemed, had a different approach to dealing with a potentially problematic leader of their shared pack.

"*This* is where the action is," the slender shifter started. "*This* is more important than whatever business I'd be taking care of back home."

Liam's words weren't overtly insubordinate, but they were enough to evoke a growl of rage from his superior. And within seconds, the lower-ranking werewolf was rattling off directions with eyes averted then obediently slipping behind the wheel of a much smaller vehicle off to one side. Apparently Gunner's worries about Ransom trumped whatever crime scene the former was going to investigate. Equally apparent—Gunner's merest hint of displeasure was law within this pack.

I was similarly shunted out of the flow of werewolves as Gunner tossed out orders to his remaining crew members. Doors slammed as half the assemblage piled into vehicles. Meanwhile, half of the shifters present spread out, trotting down the block or back into the building to form a well-oiled security patrol.

Then Liam's car was rolling away down the alley, his headlights cutting through the gloom even as other engines sprang to life on my every side. Like his departing relative, Gunner was behind the wheel of his own SUV rather than depending upon a driver. Still, the male definitely played the stereotypical alpha role as he honked his horn so loudly I instinctively jumped backwards out of the way.

Tonight was not the night for a job interview, I decided. I'd return tomorrow and beg forgiveness for the nose bleed while stating my case. In the meantime, I could brainstorm other opportunities of gainful employment. This testosterone haze of a werewolf pack couldn't be the only way to keep Kira in math books and lunch meat.

Only, Gunner hadn't forgotten about my presence. When his horn honk didn't elicit the desired reaction, the tinted window between us rolled down to expose a tense and craggy face.

"Get in," the alpha ordered, blood-encrusted nostrils flaring. He jerked his chin sideways, and for the first time I noticed that, although the back seat was cramped with three cheek-to-jowl shifters, no one had elected to ride shotgun beside their boss.

If the feeling of handcuffs around my wrists had horrified my fox instincts, entering a small space with an angry werewolf seemed akin to committing suicide. But I'd run out of good ideas and was willing to jump at the bad. So, opening the door quickly before Gunner could change his mind, I hastened to obey.

Chapter 14

We rode to the crime scene in eerie silence, sword squeezed between my knees and the rest of my body pressed up against the door. I hated being so timid, but hungry eyes lingered on the back of my neck. And every time I opened my mouth to speak, the musk of alpha werewolf coated my tongue like moss. No wonder I clamped my lips together over incipient words every time I considered breaking the ice.

Meanwhile, my star-ball-turned-sword throbbed against my pant legs, sucking heat out of the air and forming ice crystals atop everything it touched. Twice, Gunner turned the heater up a notch, and each time he eyed me with probing consideration. In response, I used the most fox-like offensive imaginable. Despite flicking glances in the predatory alpha's direction, I made sure to be looking out the window every time he returned the favor.

Finally, though, the vehicle ground to a halt just off the edge of the highway, the buffeting wind of a passing tractor trailer shaking our SUV like a leaf. This wasn't a legal place to park. But if a highway patroller dropped by, I could imagine Gunner smiling his way out of probing questions as easily as Liam had recently gotten me off the hook.

Despite our precarious parking space, the werewolf behind the steering wheel seemed in no hurry to open his door, and the shifters behind us knew better than to disembark before their boss. "It won't be pretty," Gunner informed me when we'd been sitting there long enough that my sword was beginning to create a rime of ice on plastic surfaces nine inches away. I swiped at the dashboard as unobtrusively as I could with one finger, smudging frost into water. Then I reddened as my seat mate raised his brows at the dampness coating my hand.

Before Gunner could remark upon the inconsistency, though, a mutter emerged from the peanut gallery behind our backs. "He has to warn girls first," one noted.

"Of course he does. Otherwise, they'd run screaming as soon as he unzipped his fly."

I blinked, opened my mouth...and tasted amusement replacing the former aggression in the air. Gunner's underlings were making dirty jokes about their boss now...and he wasn't tearing them to bloody pieces with his bare hands? Perhaps I didn't understand werewolves as well as I'd thought I did.

And despite everything, I found myself playing along. "I can handle ugly," I answered, blinking aside enticing mental images with an effort. No matter what his pack mates were insinuating, Gunner's warning had referred not to portions of his own anatomy but to the rotting body of a corpse. "If," I added, remembering my priorities, "it's part of the job."

"So you want it now?" Gunner's scent twisted, lightened, teased my nostrils with the humor of yet another double entendre.

"I *need* it," I countered, then reddened as the murmurs from the back seat grew even more lewd. I might have been playing along earlier, but I hadn't meant my final sentence in *that* way. At least not consciously....

Rather than trying to pry my foot out of my mouth, I pushed open my door without regard for passing vehicles...or for whatever laws of shifter hierarchy were keeping everyone else penned up inside. And for half a second I allowed myself to bask in the flow of cold air across hot cheeks, to imagine what it might feel like to be part of a pack that teased each other with such blissful simplicity while still guarding each others' backs.

Unfortunately, I wasn't a werewolf. And an innocent sister depended upon my protection both today and always. So I inhaled deeply and took in the more far-flung aromas flowing toward me beneath car-exhaust fumes. Tinges of blood and even less savory bodily fluids slapped me in the face within seconds, reminding me why I was here.

Whatever Liam had been saying about "unscented" apparently didn't apply to decomposing corpses. Shrugging, I headed down the steep slope toward the stench of death.

THE BODY WAS STUFFED beneath an overpass, subtly illuminated by the vehicle lights Gunner's pack had left on when they left their SUVs and cars. And at first glance, it looked like a homeless person had merely succumbed to the elements. Our noses, however, told us a different story entirely.

"See the baking-soda bomb?" Gunner pointed up to the bridge above our heads, where a splintered black trash bag fluttered in the breeze. Every now and then, a few white particles drifted off its otherwise pristine surface, joining the scent-leaching compound that blew around our feet like desert sand. This was a shifter-specific cover-up, a sullying of evidence that only a being with super-powered nostrils would dream of. No wonder the local pack leader's representative considered the crime his personal duty to investigate.

"Smart move on the killer's part to counteract his scent," I agreed, trying to make a good impression as I picked my way through drifts of white powder on my way to the corpse's side. Because even though crime-scene investigation didn't top my list of potential professions, I was willing to showcase relevant cleverness if that's what it took to keep Kira enrolled in her fancy private school. "Let me guess. The bag was attached to a string that could be pulled from a vehicle's window after he covered up the rest of his trail?"

"Yep," Gunner agreed, joining me as I padded closer to the victim. Even with eddies of baking soda filling the air, I could smell my companion's personal aroma now. Pine needles and ozone and dew-dampened granite, as if the male by my side embodied the type of forest I wished I could set Kira loose to frolic amidst.

I must have inhaled a little too deeply though. Because I snorted up a blend of dust and death so intense that I started sneezing wildly enough to draw tears from my eyes. Perhaps the universe was trying to tell me something....

"Alright?" Gunner asked, his hand landing lightly on my forearm. Earlier, the male had seized me so violently I couldn't get away, ripping at my sweatshirt like a boy tearing away wrapping paper on Christmas morning. But now, strength flowed from his skin into my own, the mere touch burning with so much heat it made me shiver in protest.

And even though instinct begged me to lean into the werewolf's tantalizing body, eyes on the back of my neck promised that nearby shifters were judging both of our actions. So I took a step away from the alpha's warmth instead. Swiped tears off my cheeks almost angrily.

Then I skipped over any explanation for my weakness as I peered more carefully at the waiting corpse. I was here to do a job. Might as well get it over with.

Chapter 15

The recently departed looked even more like one of the city's lost souls up close and personal. His coat was a blue so faded it had turned gray while hair streamed down his shoulders and off his chin. The man himself could have been twenty or fifty. Whatever his age, he wouldn't see another year—not now that he was quite solidly dead.

"The other body you mentioned was the same?" I asked, squashing my instinctive urge to move further away from the corpse just as I'd previously tamped down the strange attraction to the male at my side. But even though my living mother had imbued in me a healthy hesitancy about touching dead bodies, her ghost was more interested in deciphering the puzzle before our eyes.

"Three people gathering can create wisdom," Mama whispered.

And at the same moment, Gunner replied: "Same baking soda, different setting. We're looking for a serial killer now."

As he spoke, he nudged the corpse with one boot tip, toppling the body over from its side onto its back. And in response, I lost all squeamishness as my eyes took in the discordant feature shining out of the corpse's porcelain skin.

To the unmagical eye, the lost soul was likely no paler than the average dead body. After all, crime shows had informed me that when the heart ceases to beat, blood pools at the lowest point and turns the body a dusty gray.

But this corpse was paler than it should have been. Was, to the shifter eye, not just devoid of blood but lacking in magic as well.

"Like the moon and the soft-shelled turtle," Mama murmured as I dropped to my knees and pried back the scarf knotted around the dead male's throat.

Sure enough, lines of glowing magic slid down the corpse's neck and beneath his clothing. The rivulets were pulsing, tantalizing....and I unbuttoned the tattered coat nearly as roughly as Gunner had gone after my sweatshirt earlier in the day.

I wasn't expecting the resulting view though. Wasn't expecting the circle of symbols that emerged, branded upon the dead man's chest.

Or, not branded, but rather *frozen.* *"Don't try to bite your own navel,"* my mother ordered. But whatever she was obliquely warning me against, I *had* to understand what was going on.

Reaching forward, my fingers brushed against the pattern with the lightness of a feather. And, as if the magic had been waiting for me to make contact, the glowing lines coalesced into a miniature replica of a star ball before shooting comet-like into the dark. Seconds later, the dead man's chest was left as pristine as age-spotted and dirt-encrusted skin could be.

Unfortunately, I wasn't the only one who had noted the transition from magically branded to simply dead and grungy. "What was that?" Gunner demanded, hand latching down upon my unprotected nape. There was no seduction in his touch now, only hard, demanding anger. "And why did the pattern exactly match the necklace you were wearing this afternoon?"

"YOU'RE SEEING THINGS," I countered, too shaken to realize until the words left my mouth that confusion would have been a more appropriate response to his astute remark. But I hadn't expected the magical brand to be visible to the uninitiated. Meanwhile, most of my mind was intent upon figuring out how Mama's possessions could have been used to kill a man.

Because the similarity between the burnt circle and my amulet was no coincidence. In my moment of instinctive terror earlier in the day, I'd modeled the pattern of my supposed bullet-protection after one of the few objects my mother left behind her. It was easier to recreate a known pattern than to dream up something new on the fly....

Only, that particular amulet was supposed to harness good, not evil. And Mama's stories to that effect were all just superstition anyway.

Or so I'd thought at the time.

Now I sincerely regretted not having materialized a Mickey Mouse medallion as the supposed bullet blocker. Because Gunner yanked me back onto my feet with complete disregard for personal space, hands sliding from neck to shoulders as he pulled me in so close we were standing eye to eye...or rather, eye to the middle of his chest.

"You're saying it's an illusion that both your necklace thing and the burnt circle on the dead man's chest were marked with Japanese characters?" the alpha werewolf demanded. "It's an illusion that light flew off that man like a fu..." he gritted his teeth, calmed his language with an effort "...like a *freaking* ball of flame?"

Before I could answer, one of the werewolves who'd ridden in a different vehicle called toward us from the far side of the underpass. "Everything okay, boss?" Apparently our current altercation had grown loud enough to impinge upon the other werewolves' search of the surrounding landscape. And from the way the male's eyes bit into me like daggers, he agreed with Liam that a stranger shouldn't be trusted with secrets more appropriate to pack.

But Gunner was too intent upon our conversation to give his underling's warning the air space it deserved. "I'm fine. Now go," Gunner responded, biting off the words so sharply that his underling's scent of submission overwhelmed even the nearby stench of death.

Despite the clear sign that he was taking his frustration one step too far, though, the alpha's eyes never left mine even as rustlings in the bushes promised all other shifters were hastily relocating into safer territory far from potential reprimand. And, once we were even more alone than previously, the alpha's voice turned ten times quieter while its intensity ratcheted up in equal measure. "*Explain,*" he ordered for my ears alone.

The compulsion would have drawn a flood of words out of a submissive werewolf, but my fox heritage cut the command's effects down to a mere itch atop my skin. Still, I didn't like being threatened, and I didn't like the way Gunner's hands turned into manacles biting into my upper arms either. So I found myself spitting out inappropriate comments without passing the idea first by the more rational centers of my brain.

"What makes you think those are Japanese symbols? Maybe they're Chinese. Or Korean. What, you took one look at my slanty eyes and assumed I was a geisha? Racist much?"

I'd found that most Caucasians grew stymied by the assertion that prejudice colored their thinking. Gunner, unfortunately, turned out to be the exception that proved the rule. "No circles or ovals, no complicated symbols," he growled, calling my bluff with knowledge that exceeded my own. "So the symbols weren't Chinese or Korean. They were Japanese, just like you."

Japanese like all fox shifters. Japanese like the bane of werewolves' existence. I shivered, wondering for the first time whether Gunner's interest in me had ever been attraction or if he'd been suspicious of my heritage from the moment we first met.

For his part, Gunner paused for only a moment, pushing further into my personal space until his nose nearly touched my suddenly sweaty forehead. "If you have nothing to hide," my companion murmured, his gravelly voice turning almost sweet with anticipation, "then show me your necklace thing so I can compare it to what was on the dead man's chest."

As if he expected there to be blood stains on the amulet. Or for the "necklace thing" to have gone missing during the several hours in which the corpse at our feet turned from living being into so much dead meat.

Unfortunately, I couldn't think of another way to get Gunner's hands off me. He'd proven already that I couldn't outfight him once his vise-like fingers bit down. And my vulpine disinclination to being constrained was already making it hard to breathe....

So I fought to keep my inhales steady, hoping the night was dark enough to hide both the red on my cheeks and the fist-sized mass I magically yanked out of the sword sheathed by my side. Only when the amulet materialized around my neck with a near-audible pop of displaced air particles did I wince, the ice of its recently used magic burning against my skin.

"It's an *amulet*," I informed the handsy alpha, pulling the heavy circle out from beneath my clothing while subtly pushing my companion just a little further away. "And it looks nothing like what was on that dead man's chest. The symbols must have been all Japanese to you."

Gunner ignored my weak attempt at humor, and he didn't give me time to pull the chain over my head either. Instead, his huge hand swiped the amulet out of my grasp, tilting it to take in the distant glow of passing headlights while drawing my neck closer to his own. "Hmmm," he murmured, seemingly oblivious to our heart-pounding proximity.

Well, if he could stick to business then so could I. To that end, I let my gaze brush over the raised symbols that covered the amulet's surface, wishing I wasn't so sure that the hash-marked lines *did* indeed match up to the ones that had recently disappeared from the dead man's chest. But before the over-bearing alpha could debrief me further, another werewolf emerged out of the darkness inches from my left side.

"You'll want to see this, boss," the newcomer murmured, eyes narrowing only slightly as he took in my proximity to his alpha. "There's a footprint on the east side of the overpass. Scentless, small, but most definitely made by a wolf."

Chapter 16

I could feel both my job...and possibly my skin-protecting se-crets...slipping through my fingers no matter how hard I clenched said appendages into fists. Still, I stretched my legs to catch up as the two werewolves ahead of me strode up the steep hillside with complete disregard for darkness.

"I hear you, Allen," Gunner said, answering a murmur that I hadn't been able to make out as I lagged, trying to tease out the third shifter's signature scent. Allen was one of the males who'd ridden in the back seat of the SUV during the drive over, I gathered. Given how easily the trio had teased Gunner then, it was hard to imagine what might have provoked such a cool reaction from his boss now.

Giving up on the puzzle, I broke into a trot and broke out of the thicket just a step behind as the werewolves paused in an open area where a metal drainage pipe produced a flat, mud-dy area perfect for capturing passing animals' tracks. "But I've decided," Gunner continued, flicking a single glance in my di-rection that suggested I'd been the topic of conversation. Then his eyebrows rose, a clear signal that whatever conversation I'd missed was now over and done.

Shrugging, Allen got down to business, shining a flashlight between us to reveal indents of bird toes, pinpricks of insect feet...and one perfectly formed canine print just at the edge of the mud slick. The animal had traveled up the slope since the last rainfall, lacking the savvy to skirt around the muddy spot. As a result, its passing had been recorded as perfectly as any fossilized dinosaur track imprinted in Jurassic clay.

So, yes, the print definitely existed. Still, I couldn't imagine why Gunner's underling was so certain the imprint represented the foot of a werewolf. After all, its moderate size would have more closely matched a domestic canine like a Labrador retriever...or possibly a very large fox.

Did I mention that fox shifters out-mass the wild version by quite a wide margin? Kneeling down beside the track, I found my fingers stretching toward what might very well be the first sign of an unrelated fox shifter that I'd ever come in contact with.

"Don't touch that!" My hand was slapped back so abruptly I didn't even feel the sting before the shifter who had drawn us here began pointing out clues to his eagle-eyed alpha. "There's no scent," Allen informed us unnecessarily. "Note the white lines where baking soda stuck to his pads...."

"Or *her* pads," Gunner interjected, his voice so cold I cringed back away from his menacing form. Gone was the thoughtful protector who'd helped me stifle my sneezing only a few minutes earlier. Instead, Gunner had regressed into exactly the sort of terror-inducing alpha I'd assumed him to be at our first meeting.

So maybe I'd guessed wrong about Allen objecting to my presence. Perhaps Gunner was the one who wanted me gone ASAP.

"Yeah, I *guess* so," the lower-ranking shifter agreed, eyes lowered in instinctive submission as he responded to the same cues that triggered my own urge for flight. Still, the underling's tone didn't match his body language, the emphasis on "guess" suggesting he considered a female killer a profoundly unlikely hypothesis.

And after a moment of skin-saving silence, the male proved his courage by speaking up once again. "Should I run to the store for some plaster of Paris?" he asked, his voice becoming increasingly animated as Gunner's reproof faded from his memory. "I can take a casting to compare to the feet of shifters around town...."

For the first time in several minutes, I was tempted to smile. There was something so geeky about the enthusiasm infusing the underling's voice. As if arts and crafts were far more interesting than the blood and gore of a crime scene. He seemed to be envisioning a Cinderella-like hunt for our perpetrator...albeit with a much less fairy-tale ending. How surprisingly un-werewolf-like of him.

Unfortunately, Gunner shut the initiative down with the verbal equivalent of a slap. "No," the alpha growled, voice brooking no further debate. "We've learned all there is to learn here. Wrap it up and head back to base. I'm taking Mai home."

SO I GOT BACK INTO the vehicle with a surly werewolf...this time without the added buffer of teasing pack mates watching from the back seat. Only my problem wasn't the expected inability to run away from an angry alpha. Instead, Gunner opened my door like a gentleman then hesitated there on the roadside rather than slamming the barrier shut in my face.

"About earlier," he started. Then, running one hand through his hair, he shook his head as if his behavior was far too complicated to explain verbally.

"Gunner?" I asked when the silence between us had lengthened to awkward levels, half a dozen vehicles having whizzed past us on the highway. I only realized this was the first time I'd used his name aloud when my companion's scent shifted to dewy pleasure seconds before the door closed between us with a firm yet gentle snick.

Then the male was in the seat beside me, was pulling out into traffic as he headed in the direction of my neighborhood without bothering to ask where I lived. He'd clearly researched my statistics in the time we'd spent apart this afternoon. Which should have chilled me...but instead created a warm puddle of pleasure centering around the bottom of my gut.

"You need to get home to your sister," Gunner said finally, deftly switching lanes to zip past a slow-moving vehicle. "So I guess that gives us nine and a half minutes to discuss your pay rate."

"My pay rate?"

For the first time since entering the vehicle, I swiveled to face the confusing male beside me, not daring to hope that I'd heard him right. Because, possible two-sided attraction aside, I'd blown it multiple times over the course of our job-interview-turned-criminal-investigation. Why would Gunner still want me on his team?

"Funds provided for services rendered," the alpha elaborated, his tone turning honey smooth. Well, if Gunner was going to be flirtatious...then I could afford to push whatever slim advantage I might possess.

I cleared my throat then launched into the bare truth. "I need more than cash under the table," I informed him, the dour face of Kira's social worker rising up in my mind's eye. "I need a job description that sounds conventional and dependable, a weekly paycheck that I can report to Social Services. And I need seven thousand dollars on top of that, up front, to pay for Kira's school."

My requests were outrageous, but Gunner merely shrugged, taking one hand off the wheel long enough to toss his phone into my lap. "The passcode is 9653," he told me. "Text Allen and tell him what you need."

It was a good thing A came at the beginning of the alphabet, because Gunner's address book contained more contacts than I was likely to muster in ten lifetimes. Still, when I found the appropriate entry, I had to laugh. Because the plaster-of-Paris werewolf was apparently Gunner's accountant too.

"Tell him what you told me," Gunner prodded as my fingers hovered over the phone's touchscreen, unwilling to repeat my demands in print. "Five minutes until we arrive at our destination," he warned.

So I typed. I added a link to the payment portal for the academy, the email address of my least favorite social worker, and an explanation that it was me sending the text with Gunner's consent.

And the whole time I was doing so, a slender sliver of wishful thinking made me imagine what it might be like to revoke my outcast status, to have friends ready and willing to come to my aid. Perhaps that's why I knocked the previously requested seven thousand down to six thousand—surely I could come up with an extra grand from Arena fights before the deadline. It just seemed pushy to ask for so much money when my new employer was taking time out of his busy schedule to run me all the way home.

Not that the drive was a hardship in such a high-class vehicle. The faintest smile lingered on Gunner's lips when I glanced in his direction, and the SUV's brakes were silent as we pulled to a halt in front of my apartment complex seconds after I hit send. But Gunner stilled me with a hand on my arm before I could reach over to open the door and emerge from the vehicle.

"Your sister's sleeping," he noted, nodding toward the darkened window three floors above our far-too-close-together heads. "She won't know the difference if you come run with the pack tonight. I can get you home before dawn."

And with his attention turned directly upon me, the magnetism of Gunner's proximity flowed between us like the glowing magic of a star ball. I could imagine his fingers sliding across my cheekbone, his lips settling at the pulsing indentation at the base of my throat. There was so much more to this alpha than mere physical attraction. He was protective, funny, kind...

...And dangerous. So dangerous I didn't even trust myself to answer aloud as I shook my head and pushed my way out the door.

"Tomorrow then," Gunner answered before the metal barrier slipped out of my fingers and cut him off from view.

Then I was sprinting toward the dimly lit entrance of a building that suddenly felt more like a fox's underground and secretive lair than like a human's welcoming and airy residence. It took all the self-control I could muster not to turn my head and look back.

Chapter 17

I made it up two flights of stairs before the werewolves ambushed me. Was already dreaming of my sofa bed, in fact, imagining warm sheets and soft pillows while pretending there wasn't a hard bar that always ended up poking into the middle of my back. Then, in the midst of that waking hallucination, three sleek-furred four-leggers slid out of the shadows, ruffs raised and lips curled as they growled me back in the direction from which I'd come.

"Really?" I demanded, my voice a hiss as I tried to vent my displeasure without waking sleeping residents. "What do you want?"

A louder rebuttal might have done the job better. But knowing my sister, the girl would come running out of our apartment in her nightshirt if she heard a commotion. Plus, heaven forbid one of the complex's human residents stumbled out of their own residence then called the police upon sighting three wolves attacking a women so close to their home turf....

The image of Kira and cops and werewolves all mixed up into one steaming stew of catastrophe was enough to prevent me from resisting as I was herded downstairs past the entrance I'd come in through and toward the basement where a second exit opened onto the alley out back. There, though, I hesitated rather than pushing the heavy fire door open even though one of my herders lunged forward to nip at the air beside my knee.

After all, nothing good ever came out of that secluded cesspool by the dumpsters. Rushing out now with three were-wolves at my back and nothing but darkness before me felt far too much like walking into a trap....

Luckily, I was now far enough away from both sister and human residents that I could afford to make a little noise. So I resisted the wolves' nudges and peered around me instead.

On my right was the laundry room, on the left was the resident storage area, and not a single human ear was close enough to hear what was about to go down. Which meant now was the perfect time to whirl and kick out at the closest shifter, grinning when he yelped at the bruise to both his dignity and to his sensitive nose.

"Back up," I gritted from between clenched teeth, dodging just in time to bypass the shifter leaping toward my unprotected neck from the other side. So maybe these werewolves weren't just here to mess with me? Maybe they were aiming for a more final end to our engagement than that?

Well, that put an entirely different spin on matters. I hadn't been willing to indulge in full-scale battle to salvage wounded pride, but I'd do a lot to protect my own skin.

Unfortunately, half of my star ball still hung around my neck where I'd left it to avert Gunner's suspicion. Which meant the sword I pulled out of its sheathe was really only half a sword, the jagged tip menacing but the internal structure flawed by its recent loss of mass. The weapon would be as likely to shatter as to stab if I thrust it into an attacking shifter....

Of course, the three wolves leaping toward me as a single unit didn't have to know that. So I bought time with pageantry, whirling the sword in complicated circles while adding in kicks and leaps possessing no function beyond looking pretty and—I hoped—intimidating my trio of foes.

All I needed was a few seconds to strengthen the metal of my sword, a few seconds to bring its molecules back into alignment....

Ah. There.

The weapon still lacked a tip, but now it rang with resilience as I tested its prowess against one of the metal bars separating the hallway from the storage room. And my opponents must have sensed the change in my body posture, because they abruptly backed away from the true menace glinting out of my eyes.

Until, that is, the fire door disappeared behind me. And before I could dodge, a hard male arm settled vise-like across my chest.

THE SCENT OF ALPHA werewolf burned like ammonia against the exposed membranes of my nostrils, and yet I found myself relaxing rather than further tensing up. Because while this wasn't the best opponent to grab me in a near chokehold, he wasn't the worst either. "Jackal," I greeted the male behind my back.

I expected the werewolf to release me, having fulfilled whatever charade he was playing out for the sake of his men. But, instead, he pulled me in closer, the subtle slide of fingers across my fabric-covered breasts suggested I wasn't quite out of the woods just yet.

And while I was willing to go quite a distance for the sake of public appearances, groping was where I drew the line. So I pulled at my star ball's magic ever so subtly, sharpening one of the buttons on my jacket until the metal boasted a razor edge. The next time my assailant's finger slid in that general direction....

Jackal stumbled backwards, a much larger cut than I'd intended splitting open the pad of his thumb. "What the—?" he started. Then, recalling our rapt audience, he straightened from his attempt to peer at my fastener, running out his tongue instead to take one long lick along his own bleeding wound.

Within seconds, crimson stained a grinning mouthful of wolf-sharp fangs while fur sprang out in a circle around both of his eyes. The male was seconds away from shifting. And, predictably, his show of bestial dominance knocked the other werewolves off the trail of any potential weakness, sending them stumbling over each other as they retreated from us both.

I, on the other hand, had been busy figuring out how to wrangle a decent conversation without our audience turning Jackal into even more of a dick than he usually was. "If you'll excuse us for a moment...." I told the room at large, batting my eyelashes as flirtatiously as I could manage. Then I grabbed Jackal's lapels and drew him into the laundry room, kicking the door closed behind our backs. A quarter in the dryer, and soon I was confident that we could speak without being overheard.

"What do you want now?" I demanded, dropping all pretense at toadying up to the male I usually thought of as one of my few allies within my home turf. "I'm tired. Tell me whatever you have to tell me, then let me get some sleep."

I expected a request or a warning, not the ammonia-scented rage that came rolling off Jackal in waves. "You're playing with fire, pup," he told me. And even though there were no underlings present, he pushed in closer, glaring down at me with teeth that were still as sharp as any wolf's. "Being seen entering the Atwood mansion after dark then leaving with that filth. What were you thinking? No wolf waltzes in here and takes over my town and my girl."

The emphatic words rolled around in my head like so many pinballs, knocking down my defenses and abruptly pushing any soothing response out of my reach. "But it's *their* territory, not yours," I countered. "Just because they've been staying close to home for the last decade doesn't mean they don't have dibs on this land."

"If you know what's good for you, you'll change that fact," Jackal answered back just as fast. His fingers were similarly speedy when he yanked a cell phone out of his pocket, tilting the screen so I could look over the crook of his elbow and catch photo after photo of my sister's smiling face.

Kira out behind the school with no one to protect her except clawless humans. Kira walking to the corner store, a time stamp proving her expedition had occurred this evening after I'd explicitly warned her to stay at home.

The pictures were a visceral reminder that my kid sister could either be helped or harmed by this werewolf who depended upon my supposed romantic interest to solidify his precarious grasp on power. The trouble was, I couldn't just lock Kira away in her room to keep her safe.

"You've enjoyed years of protection," Jackal told me as I re-arranged my understanding of the situation, realizing too late that this male I'd thought my staunch ally was both more fickle and more dangerous than he'd initially appeared. "Now it's time for you to pony up. Get rid of those trespassers by the end of the week or I'll be forced to transfer my affections to a more malleable female. Your sister, I think, might just do the trick."

Chapter 18

Anger and fear carried me back up the same flights of stairs I'd traversed twice already in the last half hour. Rage turned my key in the apartment's lock and powered me through the darkened room on fox-soft feet. But once I tiptoed up to Kira's bed and found the girl snoring on her pillow, the events of the night all caught up with me at once.

An intriguing—and far too astute—alpha. A well-named Jackal nipping at the heels of those stronger than himself. A serial killer on the loose who appeared to possess my mother's missing possessions. And Kira, caught in the middle, with only me to defend her from the horrors of the outside world.

At least I still had my sword...and whatever information I could glean by tapping into my neighbor's unprotected wireless connection.

To that end, I booted up the laptop so ancient it had been discarded as useless by Kira's school a semester earlier. The power cord was frayed and only worked if bent at just the right angle—I folded the appropriate loop into place and tacked it down against the kitchen table with the weight of the computer itself. Similarly, the right-hand hinge was broken from being manhandled by one too many students, so I had to use two hands when opening the screen so as not to damage the machine beyond repair.

Finally, though, I had a browser in front of me, the colors blinding against the darkness of the otherwise unlit room. Tapping F9 with a fox's instinct for stealth, I continued dimming the screen until I was able to see again using my peripheral vision. Only then did I begin to type.

Luckily for me, Kira had saved passwords on the same device I was currently accessing. So it was the work of only a few minutes to discover that Mama's possessions had been sold off in three batches to three separate buyers. The closest purchaser was in Michigan, the furthest in California, and the amulet had been included in the latter lot.

It seemed hard to believe that someone had traveled halfway across the country to return items I'd considered junk to their original location then had used the self-same amulet to commit murder in a manner seemingly designed to implicate werewolves after the fact. Still, the listing was one of the few leads I'd come up with to date, so I noted down each address and Ebay handle to be analyzed once my brain was less desperately in need of sleep.

By that point, my eyelids were starting to slide closed and I knew I'd hate myself in the morning for failing to go to bed in a timely manner. Still, there were so many questions circling through my mind that I doubted my ability to sleep even if I succumbed to my current state of exhaustion.

Specifically, I wanted to know more about fox shifters, to answer the questions Kira had recently been asking. Mama had sworn me to secrecy as soon as I was old enough to say my own name, and I'd somehow carried that promise through to adulthood. But what could it hurt to google the concept and find out what the wider world knew about my kind? What would it hurt to educate myself about my abilities as well as the risks that threatened my sister and me?

So I pulled the screen closer toward me, placed my hands on the keyboard...then swore under my breath as the formerly lit surface went abruptly blank.

"I know better than that," I berated myself while fiddling with a funky hinge full of rather important cables. Had I pulled out an internal wire while trying to make the words on the screen a little easier to read? Or did the cranky laptop just need a little TLC to bring it back to life?

Only after several minutes of frustration did I realize that it wasn't the hinge that had caused the problem in the first place. Instead, my touch to the upper corner of the laptop had caused the power cord to unravel...and of course the battery no longer held a charge.

4:44 read the glowing numbers in the upper right-hand corner of the rejuvenated screen when the operating system finally booted back up. I waited for my mother to toss out a proverb about bad luck. After all, I remembered her warning me repeatedly as a child about the ill-fated nature of the number four.

But her ghost voice remained silent. So I pushed the memory aside, typing in my query with two fingers and a thumb.

"What are fox shifters?" I whispered aloud as words slowly materialized on the screen before me. And Google answered immediately, a single word popping up in a box above all other search results.

"Kitsune." The foreign word sent a jolt through the star-ball-turned-sword still scabbarded at my back. But when I nudged at my mother's ghost, she remained resolutely silent.

Well, if Mama wasn't going to explain my genealogy, then I'd have to do research on my own. Because familial secrets had already killed two innocent humans. For all I knew, Kira and I were next.

So I clicked through to the first website and slowly I began to read.

SOMETIME BEFORE DAWN, I collapsed onto the softest bed in our apartment...the one that already contained my co-matose sister. "Ge' offme," Kira complained, words running together muzzily. Then she growled sleepily as my cold fingers snuck up against her warm scalp to thaw.

"So shift," I answered only a little less groggily. There had been so many stories on the internet, myth and supposed fact and tales labeled modern fiction. Kitsune were Japanese fox shifters—that part I could vouch for myself. But were we tricksters who only appeared human in moonlight? Or beautiful and loyal women whose reflections showcased the fox within? So many stories, and none of them seemed to reference an amulet able to suck a human's life force out of his body then leave said two-legger with a miniature star ball frozen into his chest.

So I took the easy way out and decided to deal with my heritage tomorrow. Instead of mulling over the issue further, I snuggled closer to my sister, waiting for her to pull upon her fur form and make a little extra space for me on the bed. After all, the bar in the sofa bed was brutal. I ended up here more often than not, and Kira was always willing to shift and snuggle.

Only, apparently, she was feeling argumentative tonight. "*You* shift," my sister countered, sounding more awake than previously as she elbowed me in the kidneys. Her bones were sharp and her tone was surprisingly adamant, so this time I shrugged and obeyed.

One moment I was a women frozen and exhausted, mind running in endless circles that all centered around the child hugged within my arms. The next, I was a fox, moist nose the only part of me exposed to the chilly air in our barely-heated apartment. Tucking my snout beneath my tail solved that problem, and soon I was as toasty as if Kira had let me under the covers in the first place. This was the life....

With that thought, I drifted off and slept the sleep of an innocent animal. The bed was soft, my sister was close, and vague threats could be dealt with at a later date.

Too bad "later" came far too prematurely when the kitchen door crashed open and werewolves poured into our previously solitary den.

Chapter 19

Laptop, fox, sister. Three potential weaknesses, none of which I could currently guard against displaying to the outside world. Not when my own body represented the second danger, my red fur glimmering in the full-noon sunlight that bathed our small but well-lit room.

Kira, on the other hand, was currently human and quite capable of diving directly into muddy waters without measuring the distance to rock bottom first. "What are you doing here?" she demanded while stalking toward our uninvited guests in half-dressed tween splendor. "Have you ever heard of knocking? Didn't you realize a locked door means *Keep out?*"

I itched to protect rather than hide and continue being protected, but rationality pushed me flat against the bed instead. Because if these werewolves became aware of my identity, they'd know what Kira was as well....

A heart that always beat faster in vulpine form now pounded so hard against my throat that I could barely breathe. Meanwhile, the rumpled covers that stood between me and discovery felt far thinner than they had in the darkness last night.

Kira, get back here! I wanted to scream the words, wanted to drag my sister out of harm's way. But all I actually managed was a twitch of my whiskers before an unexpectedly familiar voice soothed the worst of the terror out of my skin.

"I apologize, ma'am." I sighed out the reediest whine of relief as I realized this was Allen, Gunner's geekiest assistant. Still a werewolf and perhaps suspicious of me...but at least not currently slavering after my blood.

"We tried to call and we tried to knock," the male continued, unaware of my near meltdown, "but there was no answer. Gunner was concerned something might have happened, so he gave us permission to force entry. If you want to put on some clothes and get your sister, we'll wait...."

Terror gradually gave way to curiosity, allowing me to sniff the air and assess the situation more fully. Astonishingly, embarrassment was the key emotion rolling off these home-invading werewolves. So I risked a peek around a corner of my cover barricade, noting the way Allen looked at everything other than my sister while his cheeks turned from faintly flushed to boiled-beet red.

Aw. A baby-doll nightie on an underage female was apparently a better weapon than the one I itched to grasp into my not-yet-present hand. Kira *was* rather well developed for a twelve year old....

Still, Allen wasn't the only werewolf present. There were two bulky shifters behind him, one of whom seemed far more interested in his cell phone than in his surroundings. The other, though, was nosing around the laptop I'd been using as night faded into morning, the exact same device I couldn't quite remember shutting down properly before I stumbled off to bed.

Had the browser still been up when I abandoned the computer? Would the screen flicker to life full of damning evidence if Nosy's fingers hit the proper key sequence? Now more than ever, I needed Kira to close the bedroom door so I could regain my humanity and shut this party down....

And as if I'd called her attention to me by the force of willpower alone, my sister swiveled slightly to glance in my direction. Then her head tilted in a query I hoped was too subtle for the werewolves to make out.

The door, I tried to communicate with widened eyes and flaring nostrils. And the motion must have caught Allen's attention, because he took a step forward...only to disappear from view as Kira got the message and slammed the much-needed barrier between uninvited werewolves and myself.

"Mai's in the bathroom," my sister prattled as I yanked hard on my magic, shifting in less than a second into shivering human form. *Clothes, clothes, clothes,* I reminded myself, hopping into yesterday's wrinkled outerwear without bothering to don undergarments first. After all, forming the brilliant ball of frigid magic currently streaming out of my body into sword form was more important than panties if my goal was rushing to my sister's aid.

"Nobody's in *this* bathroom," Allen was saying as I pushed my way out into the kitchen-living-room combo.

"Well, we've got two," my sister lied through her teeth.

And before the accountant could argue about the unlikelihood of a one-bedroom, two-bathroom apartment, I was shoving my sister behind my back and slamming the laptop screen down inches from Nosy's furtive fingers. I think I heard the hinge crack all the way through in the process. But as best I could tell, no secrets had as yet been revealed.

"I'm here. My sister is none of your business," I told them. Then, dividing my glare equally between all three werewolf faces: "Now get out of our house."

"THIS ISN'T A HOUSE, actually," Allen countered. "More like an apartment. Or, if you're British, a flat."

"Your lips are moving but your feet aren't," I observed, doing my best to usher all three werewolves toward the open door via physical intimidation alone. Unfortunately, Allen was the smallest of the three shifters and even he topped me by a good six inches at a conservative guess. No wonder none of the werewolves budged in response to my attempted loom.

The phone-obsessed shifter, on the other hand, *did* deign to speak...even though his eyes remained glued to his cell screen. "Boss says to tell chica here that he's tied up at the moment but that he'll see her this evening. In the meantime, she's in charge of the investigation today."

I was in charge of three home-breaking werewolves? Something didn't quite add up. "What were Gunner's exact words?" I demanded, angling closer in hopes I could see what was so engrossing about that tiny screen.

"I don't think..." Phone Dude hemmed. At which point Nosy snatched the device out of his pack mate's hand and read the contents aloud.

"*Tell Mai I'm busy measuring my brother's cock. Back tonight. Until then, she's the boss.*"

"Told you it wasn't appropriate for the ears of a lady," Phone Dude grumbled.

"What could be more appropriate for a lady than cock measuring?" Nosy countered.

"Crow, Tank, that's *enough*."

And while I should have been laughing right along with Kira at Allen's attempt to squash his pack mates' hilarity, something warm began unfurling in my stomach instead.

"You know what they say about a guy with small feet," I'd teased two nights prior at the Arena. No wonder Gunner had turned so grumpy yesterday evening when we stumbled across an extra-small canine track near the site of the murder. Had the alpha really taken my jab so literally? And if he believed Ransom to be responsible for the killing...why would Gunner risk his most important relationship by relaying that information to a near stranger like me?

Those questions could be dealt with later. For now—"If I'm in charge, then let's investigate," I said at last, trying not to read too much into Gunner's show of trust. Yet again, I waved my hands toward the still-open door leading into the hallway...and yet again no one bothered to so much as shuffle their feet in the indicated direction.

"Sure thing, bossette," Nosy—aka Crow—answered. "Just tell us who's gonna stay here to take care of the kid and the rest of us will be on our way."

As I glanced at three waiting faces, I realized this must have been yet another order meted out by their absent leader. And while I would have scoffed at Gunner's over-protectiveness yesterday, in light of Jackal's recent comments I found myself both relieved and ready to accept.

"Allen can stay," I decided, figuring the smartest werewolf was also the one least likely to lose track of Kira if she got it into her head to play hide and seek with her bodyguard. Then, turning to my sister, I laid down the law. "You've got enough homework to keep you busy all day," I informed her. "I want to see you parked on the sofa when I get home."

Kira glanced at me, raised an eyebrow, then turned the full force of her charm upon her designated keeper. "Wanna learn a magic trick?" she asked Allen, tilting her head down until she was peering up from between dark lashes. "I'm excellent at making things disappear."

I turned to the door to hide my smile. Allen would be lucky if he made it out of this babysitting session with wallet and dignity intact.

Chapter 20

I didn't remember what day it was until hours later. Friday. The last work day of the week, when fights began early and crowds at the Arena doubled in size. I couldn't afford to miss the match this evening, not when the whole point of Wednesday's loss had been setting up a resounding Friday win.

Which gave me a limited window in which to discharge the duties of my new day job then get rid of Tank and Crow. Unfortunately, neither task looked like it was going to be easy to accomplish in haste.

"Well that was a waste of time," I groused once we'd finished nosing around the crime-scene site a second time and had returned to cruising down random city streets. Given the lack of information found at the now-cleaned-up underpass, I was beginning to think Gunner had hoped I'd spend the day spinning my wheels with the sole purpose of taking the heat off his own spur-of-the-moment trip.

And I would have been glad to oblige if I'd thought Ransom was the culprit. Unfortunately, that conclusion seemed dramatically premature. From the little bit I'd seen of the Atwood pack leader, Ransom was hotheaded and not a terribly good fighter...but none of that added up to a serial killer using Ebay-purchased heirlooms to somehow magic humans to death. I mean—what was the point? And did Ransom really possess the gumption to figure out a puzzle that continued to elude my own grasp?

Not likely. Which meant there was an actual miscreant on the loose in my city. And from the way Tank and Crow peered at me like puppy dogs expecting their master to pull a bag of treats out of her pocket, it was up to me to guide the exploration onto the proper path.

"I think we should take a look at the original body," I decided aloud, feeling my way through potential alternative avenues of investigation. After all, what better way to track down the twisted personality we were seeking than to assess his initial foray into life taking? Maybe there was a magical signature on his body that the werewolves had missed....

Unfortunately, my supposed backup turned into minders as soon as I spat out an actual game plan. "No can do," Crow said tersely, swinging into a fast-food drive-through. Then, completely changing the subject from what we were meant to be discussing: "Anybody else want a snack?"

Tank looked up from his cell phone long enough to shoot off a list of items that amounted to half a cow plus an extra-large potato field. Crow ordered all of the above plus enough sugar to rot out his teeth. And I tacked on a grilled chicken sandwich, hold the mayonnaise, plus a large ice water on the side.

"What?" I demanded once we were parked and eating. Or, rather, once *I* was eating. The guys just stared at me from beneath their mountains of food as if I'd grown an extra arm.

"You don't have to pretend to be human around us, chica," Tank told me after a moment. He patted me on the head as if *I* was the puppy...which made it hard not to snap at his patronizing hand.

"Here, have some of my fries," Crow added, holding out the cardboard carton...then pulling it back before I had time to so much as shake my head. "Or...Tank can go back in and get you your own fries maybe. Boss won't be happy if you faint from lack of food."

I scrunched my eyes shut, astonished at how drastically the reality of werewolves differed from my expectations. Here I'd spent decades shivering at werewolf shadows only to find that the sole threat from their presence was death by frustration...or perhaps exploding when I followed their lead and ate way too much.

"I have food," I growled once I finally trusted myself enough to speak. Then, remembering what I'd asked before Crow sidetracked me, I pressed my earlier point. "We *can't* go see the body? Or you *won't* take me there?"

"Can't," Tank answered.

"Won't," Crow added.

Both males spoke with their mouths full, and I had to avert my eyes before I was willing to take a bite of my own lunch. "Explain," I ordered after chewing and swallowing. Single words sometimes worked with Kira. Perhaps similar simplicity would do the trick while attempting to whip my unlikely assistants into shape.

Sure enough, the males seemed willing enough to expand upon their earlier answers when pinned down. "We disposed of it," Tank elaborated. "Weighed it down and sunk it in the middle of the river. Can't have pesky bodies floating around for the human cops to find."

"Plus, the boss said to keep you safe," Crow added once his partner had finished. "First murder was two weeks ago. That corpse has moved on from dead to wrigglin', if you know what I mean."

I *did* know what he meant. And suddenly the grainy texture of the reconstituted chicken meat in front of me looked far too much like maggots for my peace of mind.

Closing the paper wrapper back up around the rest of my sandwich, I did my best to hold onto my temper. "So what *are* we allowed to do today?"

"Investigate," Crow answered.

"Drive around and look for shit," Tank suggested.

The pair had somehow managed to scarf down 99% of their lunch while I was nibbling through a quarter of my own small meal. Now, Crow pulled back onto the road, one last double bacon cheeseburger in his hand...well, until he shoved the entire thing into his mouth that is. "Where to, bossette?" the long-haired shifter asked around chunks of beef and pork.

As if I was the one actually in charge of this disaster. And as if we weren't wasting precious hours when I had better things to do...like preparing for a very lucrative fight.

"Turn right," I decided. "Then left at the stoplight...."

In short order, I'd found what I was looking for. A thoroughfare so packed that parking was unlikely within a ten-block radius. Even slowing down here would risk the driver's life...or at least the structural integrity of his wheels.

Which is when I opened my door and leapt from the moving vehicle, ignoring the shouts of distress behind me and the blaring of nearby horns. Sprinting for an alley, I barely caught

Tank's recriminations before I shook the pesky babysitters off my tail.

"Chica! The boss won't like this!" the burly shifter howled.

But "the boss" was far too engrossed in determining whether his brother was a murderer to worry about me at the moment. So I slipped behind the awning of a bustling street cafe, ran down a set up steps, sprang over a wall, and was soon back within my comfort zone—entirely on my own.

Chapter 21

"She who chases two rabbits catches neither."

"And she who talks to the voices in her head gets locked up," I muttered back to my mother's ghost as I wound my way through the unsavory streets of the Warren on the way to my ultimate goal. I'd tugged on as many investigative threads as possible without straying far from my path over the last couple of hours. And, no, I hadn't come up with any blinding flashes of insight in the process. But it was better than trying to do the same work while dragging around two gruffly overprotective werewolves. Plus, I still held out hope that some of the seeds I'd planted might bear fruit...after the upcoming fight.

Now I paused in a shadowy alcove just outside the Arena, hasty fingers running through tangled hair while my magical senses performed the more important preparation—materializing my sword within the sheathe along my spine. The match was due to begin in a matter of minutes, and I didn't need a Japanese proverb to know I'd better get my head into the game before dashing through that door.

So, pushing away Mama's memory, I closed my eyes and focused on Dad's voice instead. My father had fought in the Arena as long as I could remember, and he'd passed along many of his tricks to me. The most important, he'd always asserted, was preparation. *"Before you start fighting,"* he'd always told me, *"remember to center on your breath."*

Closing my eyes now, I obeyed the oft-repeated admonition. Sucked in a deep lungful of air through my nose then gently relaxed the carbon dioxide away between loosely parted teeth. Whoever Ma Scrubbs had chosen as today's opponent would be more bark than bite. As long as I ignored their bluster, chances were good that I'd win...and pay the rest of Kira's tuition in the process.

"Darkness lies one inch in front of your nose."

My eyelids burst open at Mama's shrill interjection, breath coming faster as I peered around the dim alley in search of potential danger. Her words had seemed so ominous at first blush...but now that I thought about it, I was pretty sure that proverb was merely telling me to expect the unexpected. Perhaps this was Ghost Mama's attempt to help out?

Whatever the reason, I wasn't quite in the zone when I slipped in the back entrance of the Arena moments later. Sure, my sword was in my hand and my muscles were loose and ready. But the roar of the crowd made me wince as I left the shadows behind and walked out under the blinding floodlights.

Meanwhile, the words of the announcer didn't help matters either. "Please welcome Wednesday's competitors back to the Arena! Ladies and gentleman, introducing Mai Fairchild and Ransom Atwood!"

IT WASN'T RANSOM, THOUGH, who appeared on the other side of the small cage as my eyes adjusted to the over-illumination. Instead, resembling his brother enough to make the false identity work from a distance, Gunner greeted me with a grin that did odd things to my stomach. Then, taking advantage of my unconscious lean in his general direction, my opponent opened the fight with a forward lunge transitioning into a slashing stroke of the sword clasped in one long-fingered fist.

In response, I dropped to the ground and somersaulted past him, rolling upwards even as the alpha spun to trace my path. I told myself it was just Mama's unhelpful words of encouragement that made Gunner's reappearance hit me like a punch to the gut the moment I set eyes upon him. But his verbal greeting both deepened my reaction and illuminated my lie.

"I was worried," the big, scary alpha told me, a subtle tightening around his eyes suggesting he was actually telling the truth even though his sword continued to parry mine stroke for stroke. "Crow and Tank called two hours ago. Said you'd slipped your leash. The whole pack's been tearing the city apart ever since. I figured you could take care of yourself. But..."—he feinted then struck at my knees, a blow I easily blocked—"...I'm glad to see your face."

"Aw, you missed me," I countered, finding it easy to keep my words light when my feet felt as if they were walking on rainbows. Taking advantage of the emotion-fueled energy, in fact, I transitioned into one of Dad's favorite combo moves then. Bing, bang, boom. Feint, parry, attack. Gunner must have had more experience with swordsmanship than I'd expected or he would have ended up with a game-ending scratch right then.

Instead, the male proved his prowess by nearly catching me on the rebound, swiping low a second time and forcing me to leap to evade his sword. "I did miss you," he agreed, not even out of breath as he offered a stab that could easily have pierced my stomach lining. "And I'm glad to be back. Not least because we have a mystery to solve."

I inhaled as I twisted sideways, windmilling my arms then using the change in balance to launch my own attack. "I could have told you Ransom's feet weren't that little," I puffed, finally losing a bit of my composure as Gunner's blade caught mine and nearly ripped said object out of my grasp.

The scrape of metal against metal provoked a cheer from bystanders I'd nearly forgotten, widening my tunnel vision at last. The crowd members were standing on their seats now, pounding fists against the cage that locked me and Gunner in. Calls of "Ransom" and "Mai" rang out across the Arena in equal measure, and I wasted half a second hoping Ma Scrubbs was right and fewer watchers had bet in my favor this time around.

Because I was going to win. Never mind what a smirking Gunner thought as a flick of his wrist ripped my sword away to send it flying toward the chain link behind my back. My opponent might be bigger and stronger. But I needed the cash far more than he did...and I'd never promised to fight fair.

So even as the sword left my fingers, I sucked as hard as I could against the retreating magic, feeling icy tentacles sliding into the darkness up my sleeve. The shell of my former weapon clanged dully against the cage wall even as I formed a slightly smaller rapier in the same sheathe the original sword had occupied five minutes earlier.

"Never bet against a Fairchild," I told Gunner. At the same time, I reached behind my back to grab the replacement blade even as I danced forward to swipe the tiniest pinprick of a line above my opponent's brow.

If he'd seen the move coming, he could have dodged or even parried. But Gunner had thought I was out of weapons. So he stood like a rock, the widening of his eyes nearly as satisfying as the adulation of the crowd.

Unlike Gunner, I knew how to play to my audience. So I turned, bowed, turned again. And I would have bowed yet another time had I not caught a glimpse of an unexpectedly familiar face pressing up against the chain-link door.

"*She's gone*," Allen mouthed, face as white as mine was suddenly growing. The accountant didn't need to elaborate for me to realize he referred to the girl I'd left in his charge several hours earlier.

Someone had snatched Kira right out from under my nose.

Chapter 22

"Mai, wait!"

I ignored both Gunner's command and the rational knowledge that my sister might have just slipped her leash the same way I'd done a few hours earlier. Because I trusted my gut, and my gut told me Kira wouldn't risk throwing off my game on fight night just because she felt cooped up in our apartment with a werewolf babysitter.

No, if Allen was unable to find my sister, that meant someone had taken the child against her will.

So, delaying only long enough to swipe my now-hollow sword off the ground, I sprinted out of the cage and toward the nearest exit. Behind me, I could hear the alpha debriefing his underling. And while Allen's quiet words were swallowed up by the noise of the crowd, I didn't need to hear answers to Gunner's increasingly frantic "Where?" and "Who?" and "How do you know?" to send me in the right direction.

Jackal had threatened my sister yesterday and now Kira had disappeared. I knew precisely where to look to get her back.

Getting there, however, was another matter entirely. Hard elbows and heavy feet pummeled my extremities as I forced my way through a sea of human bodies that seemed uninterested in parting to let me through. And for once, I regretted being smaller than average. Because one glance over my shoulder proved that Gunner was having no problem keeping pace, the werewolf's bulk preventing the tide of humanity from sucking him under the way it threatened to do me. Too bad he wasn't willing to act as a battering ram to help me achieve my destination in a timely manner.

In fact, Gunner was not only failing to help, he was actively working against me. Or so it seemed seconds later when raised hairs on the back of my neck proved that the alpha had closed the gap between us just as a hand on my shoulder swung me around to face back in the direction from which I'd come.

"Mai, I know you're worried. But you can't run off half-cocked before we figure out what's happening...."

Werewolf platitudes. I bared my teeth, wondering if the surprise of fangs piercing flesh would be enough to remove the restraining hand so I could continue on my way....

Then a human larger even than Gunner was looming over me. The newcomer's bulk pushed the alpha backwards before the latter even realized what was happening, at which point a wad of folded bills slipped from the human's fingers into my own beneath the eddies of the crowd.

"She doesn't need to talk to me?" I asked the doorman, surprised that Ma Scrubbs was resisting her usual impulse to haggle me down from our agreed-upon percentage. Tonight, though, the sheets of doubled-over paper were an inch thick. And, for once, I had more important matters at hand than pinching pennies and counting every bill.

So I accepted the doorman's silence as implicit agreement then turned and sped through the open tunnel he'd left behind him as he pushed his way through the crowd to reach my side. Breaking out into the alley at last, I breathed in one huge gulp of much-needed oxygen. And, finally, I turned to face the alpha who I still hadn't managed to shake off my tail.

Which, apparently, was a good thing. Because no matter how I poked at the issue, one fox shifter against a couple dozen werewolves wasn't good odds for freeing my sister. So I closed my eyes, sighed, and accepted the inevitable.

"I need your help," I admitted. "Your help, and the help of your most trustworthy men."

"*These* are your most trustworthy men?"

"*This* is where you think your sister is being held?"

We were talking at cross-purposes...and, honestly, I could see Gunner's point. The local Walmart didn't top most were-wolves' lists for hostage-negotiation venues. Of course, Jackal wasn't most werewolves either.

Still...Tank, Crow, and Allen were Gunner's chosen back-up? I'd thought the Atwood pack's second-in-command was able to call upon more skilled manpower than the three odd-balls he'd sent to my apartment to wake me earlier in the day. If I'd known we were going in with jokers as backup, I would have skipped negotiating with werewolves and instead hired a pair of human fighters off the street.

Because all I really needed for this job was two dependable allies. Too bad I wasn't so sure any of my companions were up to the task.

"I trust Tank, Crow, and Allen with my life," Gunner said levelly as he and his trio of pack mates followed me through Walmart's automatic doors, past the pharmacy section, and out into the open air of the screened-in garden center. "I don't think you heard Allen's full report, though. He lost Kira at the cemetery...."

Willingly, the spectacled werewolf began repeating the same story I'd gathered from bits and pieces tossed out during the rush to reach our current location. Since I'd already guessed the details before I heard them, though, I tuned out the male's repetition and began navigating by scent alone.

Not many people visited the garden center in early March, so I wasn't surprised to be able to pick out Jackal's trail as easily as ever. Actually, there were half a dozen pathways leading to the same location, the amount of time the male spent browsing likely dependent upon how many humans were around when he initially arrived.

And, sure enough, the freshest trail had been made mere hours earlier. No sign of Kira, but it was hard to get a handle on what exactly had happened with dozens of bags of mulch and fertilizer exuding their own overwhelming scents. I forced myself not to dream up reasons my sister's aroma might be absent, but the baking-soda-influenced paw print at the crime scene rose unerringly into my mind without my consent. If anyone had small feet, that someone would be a pack-leader-wannabe like Jackal....

"Mai, you're not even listening." Gunner was in front of me now, a wall of alpha preventing me from prying up the loose flagstone that covered the tunnel to Jackal's lair. I'd found this spot years earlier when the male first came courting, his honey-eyed words prompting me to tail my supposed paramour and figure out what made him tick. What I'd discovered was an underground chamber accessed via Walmart's garden center, the place he went to be alone. Since Jackal apparently thought he was the only one aware of the den's existence, this seemed like the perfect spot to stash a girl he wanted no one else to discover.

Unfortunately, there was currently an alpha werewolf standing between me and my intended destination. Meanwhile, hair-raising electricity proved that Gunner's patience was wearing thin. "Mai," he growled so intently that I gave in and wasted thirty precious seconds getting the doubter off my back.

"Kira wanted to go to the cemetery," I recited, repeating Allen's words back to them in a much condensed form. "To the pond in the middle with the huge weeping willow and the spring-fed waterfall covered in moss. That's where she always wants to go. That's where we spread our father's ashes."

"I'm sorry." The tremendous werewolf before me deflated visibly...which just made me madder since his pity was wasting yet more time during which my sister was stuck beneath our feet terrified and hopefully alone.

"Allen let her play hide and seek," I continued, managing the barest hint of a smile for the accountant-turned-babysitter who was clearly berating himself for losing track of his charge. Now that I took in my entire audience, I realized Gunner was forcing this issue for more than my sake. Allen needed to be let off the hook if he was going to be any use during the battle ahead.

"It was clever, Allen," I continued. "Don't let your boss tell you otherwise. Making Kira finish one math problem every quarter hour was a good way to keep her on track and ensure she was still hanging around while giving her a bit of breathing space at the same time. Kira doesn't like being forced to sit still and she *loves* disappearing into that tree."

Despite my words, the male in question still hung his head. "I should have kept a closer eye on her...."

"You did nothing wrong," I said honestly. "Someone snatched my sister. And now we're going to get her back."

I turned around then to face that all-important flagstone, ready to push Gunner out of the way if necessary. But it turned out my words had achieved their original goal as well as softening Allen's penchant toward self-chastisement. Because the argumentative alpha was no longer standing atop the hidden entrance, and he even knelt down to help me slide the covering aside without being asked.

The hole we revealed was barely large enough to crawl through, dirt-lined and dark as far as the eye could see. Predictably, my fox nature perked up at the close, dank confines. The wolves behind me, on the other hand, sucked in one united, claustrophobic breath.

"This is why you didn't want more backup," Gunner murmured. Like me, he was now understanding that whoever waited on the other end of the tunnel could pick off invaders at his leisure. There was no point in bringing an army to a battle that, by necessity, had to be fought one on one. I needed a single dependable wolf at my back and a few more guarding the exit. After that, the battle would turn on skill level alone....

"Correct," I answered. Then, drawing my sword, I dove into the tunnel before Gunner was able to start an argument about who'd go through first.

Chapter 23

The tunnel was worn smooth by repeated passage, but dirt still scraped off the ceiling from time to time and filtered through my hair. I ignored the itch, however, trying instead to figure out why I couldn't smell my sister's distinctive odor no matter how hard I sniffed.

Would Jackal have pushed his prisoner or pulled her? The male was lazy, I reasoned, so he'd likely kept Kira conscious so she could crawl into the darkness under her own volition. Still, my ferocious sister would have fought rather than giving in easily. She would have clawed, maybe even shifted form and bit at her captor's hand. So why hadn't her efforts left behind traces of her existence? Why didn't I smell even the faintest hint of blood?

Behind us, the scrape of stone on pavement coincided with the extinguishing of the last faint glimmer of light shining over my shoulder. And, in response, my star ball pulsed against my fingers, begging to be let out of its weaponized form so it could illuminate the pathway ahead.

"Mai?" Werewolf fingers closed around my ankle and a shiver ran up my spine. But the reaction wasn't terror. Instead, Gunner's warmth gave me the courage to continue crawling forward into the darkness, holding my star ball's illuminatory impulses in check. After all, we couldn't risk alerting Jackal to our impending entrance with a blaze of magical starlight. Our only real chance was to burst out of the hole so quickly our opponent lacked all opportunity to block the gap....

"If you do not enter the tiger's cave, you will not catch its cub," Mama murmured. And this time my skull thunked into the top of the tunnel in reaction to the ghost's sudden arrival inside my mind.

"Now isn't a good time for proverbs," I retorted...then cringed as I smelled Gunner's interest behind my back. There would be questions later, I gathered. For now, all I could manage was to push onward while ignoring both my mother's talkative ghost and the fact that I was willingly leading one very powerful alpha werewolf toward a sister who might currently inhabit the skin of a fox.

It felt like we crawled for hours after that. The space heated and dampened around us, and my pupils dilated so dramatically they began to strain against the absence of light. Then I pushed my sword forward just as I'd done a second earlier and a second before that...and the weapon slipped away from me, crashing against a hard surface within a much larger room.

Was Kira sitting with that darkness scared out of her mind by the clatter? Or was Jackal lying in wait beside his captive, crouched and smiling as he used the lack of illumination to give him the upper hand?

My sword, unfortunately, had taken the element of surprise out of our court already. So I didn't assess the danger further. Just pushed myself out of the hole with all my might, rolling sideways as I snatched at where I guessed the blade had fallen.

And it was a good thing my star ball refused to cut me or I would have ended up with a gash through my right palm to match the scab on my left. As it was, I banged my shin hard against a chair leg as I came to standing then spun in a circle as light emerged from behind my back.

"It's me," Gunner grunted as my blade cut through the air half a centimeter from his cell-phone-turned-flashlight. Not bothering to defend himself further, he lifted the device above his head and looked around.

Together, we took in a lair well furnished with stolen Walmart chic. Just like last time, the space was clean and almost cozy...if you ignored the cave crickets and spiders crawling across the uneven floor. There were rugs atop the dirt, a folded chair plus a mound of pillows in one corner, even an electric camp stove off to one side.

Unfortunately, the space was also entirely empty of anyone except me and Gunner. Neither my sister nor Jackal was there.

GUNNER RAISED ONE EYEBROW as he took in my shock and devastation. I'd been so sure Kira would be here to greet me. Had been so sure that saving her skin was worth risking our secret around this far too astute werewolf...who was even now opening his mouth to begin a debrief I couldn't afford.

But before my companion could spit out a single word, a werewolf leapt out of the tunnel behind us, shifting midair so he landed naked but human by his alpha's side. "Jackal's been sighted on the other side of the city," Crow reported, holding out a cell phone he'd carried through the tunnel in his lupine mouth. The device was wet with spittle, but I grabbed it before

Gunner could close his fingers around the damp plastic. Then I peered down at the picture on the screen.

Jackal in his home turf. Two shifters I didn't recognize behind his left shoulder. No sign of my sister in sight.

"If we go into the Warren after him, he'll slip through our fingers," I observed, already considering the hundreds of exit points surrounding the city's underbelly. "He could have stashed Kira anywhere. We'll have to tempt him out by offering something in exchange."

But what? Myself as mate was the only obvious bargaining chip, but Jackal had clearly tired of sniffing after me. What he wanted was territorial rights to the city...something an alpha werewolf like Gunner would never provide.

As if reading my mind, Gunner smiled faintly. "I can think of several somethings Jackal would like to have. None of which he's getting. But it won't hurt to pretend."

The alpha nodded his chin toward the tunnel then, and Crow shivered down into lupine form before leaping back into the small space he'd come in through. Only after we were once more alone in the otherwise empty lair did Gunner take a step toward me, bending over slightly so he could peer more intently into my eyes.

"I need to understand the bigger picture if I'm going to help your sister," my companion rumbled, his voice so deep it vibrated against my bones. His proximity felt like sticking my finger into an electric socket while teetering above a bathtub—a burst of shock and awareness wrapped up in the knowledge that even greater danger lay mere inches away.

In response, I tried—and failed—to pry my lips open, expecting every minute for the male to push harder against my obvious reservations. After all, he was an alpha werewolf, used to taking whatever he wanted. And even though my fox nature made verbal compulsions roll off my back like so much rainwater, my milk-money debt worked in the opposite direction, urging me to give this particular werewolf anything he cared to request.

The wave-like crash was almost audible as the inconsistencies in my various stories collided together in Jackal's abandoned den. Lies, lies, and more lies leading to questions beyond my ability to brush off. Like—how did my half-Japanese heritage relate to the murderer on the loose in our city? And why did my sister and I choose to live on our own when female werewolves would have been welcomed with open arms by any pack...

...assuming, that is, I was actually a werewolf and that my sister was the same.

Rather than voicing the obvious, though, Gunner merely stood over me and waited. His scent embraced my body, clearing my sinuses and at the same time tightening my chest until I could barely breathe.

And as if in response to that two-sided reaction, my star ball disobeyed my earlier commandment and began glowing gently. It was only the faintest flicker of illumination, and Gunner now held two cell phones to beat back the darkness. Still, I knew he noticed when the scent in the den turned from salty dominance into spicy intrigue.

"Mai?" the male murmured at last. "Is there something going on with your sword?"

I couldn't answer, but I also couldn't lie while my debt held me within its power. So I broke the moment in the only way I was capable of. I ignored the way his gaze raised hairs up and down my spine, stashed my disobedient weapon away beneath my clothing, then padded toward the tunnel in three quick strides. After that, I crawled into the hole so quickly I bruised both elbows and knees against the hard earthen ground.

Gunner slipped in right behind me, his broad shoulders catching on the walls and slowing him down in areas where I could slither straight on through. Still, I didn't take advantage of the opportunity to flee when I emerged amid a ring of interested faces.

After all, while Gunner might suspect everything, he knew nothing. And until Kira was safe, the watchful werewolf was still the best ally I currently had on hand.

Chapter 24

" *The talented hawk hides its claws,*" my mother noted as Gunner's SUV pulled to a halt in front of my apartment complex. And despite my best attempt at maintaining a poker face, I was pretty sure I jolted visibly at the internal commentary yet again. So it was a good thing any astute alpha questions were cut off by an interjection from the back seat.

"One hour," Tank informed us, looking up from his phone for the first time since we'd entered the vehicle. "Jackal says he'll meet us at the southside McDonald's at 11 pm. He wants Mai there."

I nodded, already pushing open the SUV door in relief. I'd be too frazzled to think straight if I spent the next sixty minutes in these wolves' presence...especially with the ghost of a mother hovering at the back of my mind. So a little time to stuff Mama back in the corner where she belonged—and to finally pull on a pair of panties to stop the chaffing—seemed like a gift from the gods.

Unfortunately, a hand reached out to close around my left wrist before I could make good on my escape. "You're not going to run," Gunner informed me, the words a question disguised as an order.

"I just need time to shower and catch my breath," I replied honestly. Well, that, plus the leeway to pull my brain back together. Mental hygiene, physical hygiene—it amounted to pretty much the same thing. "I'll meet you there."

"We'll pick you up," Gunner countered, but he *did* release my wrist. And even though I could feel the alpha's eyes boring into my back as I strode to the apartment building's entrance, the vehicle was gone when I peered back through the fogged glass from inside.

Only then did I lean my forehead against the tiny square of window, close my eyes, and speak to the ghost who seemed intent upon hounding my every move. "Any ideas, Mama? On how to get Kira back?"

"A frog in a well does not know..." my mother began, only to lapse into silence rather than finishing the phrase.

"Doesn't know what, Mama?"

I was talking to myself in an empty stairwell, I realized as I spun in a circle hoping for more words of wisdom from someone who had died soon after Kira was born. Despite that self-awareness, however, I waited longer than I cared to consider, hoping the ghost would return and at least finish her sentence if nothing else.

But, at last, I was forced to admit my solitude. So I walked up the stairs alone, padded down the hallway with my hand on my star-ball-turned-sword...then froze as I took in a small rectangle of paper tacked to the outside of my apartment door.

FOR HALF A SECOND, I thought Kira had come back and left me a note so I wouldn't worry. That she'd just been teasing Allen, had forgotten tonight was fight night, had let her mercurial fox nature get the better of her considerate human mind.

Then I stepped closer, took in scrawled handwriting nothing like my sister's looping script. Knew Kira was well and truly taken and wasn't going to be returned easily or willingly to her home.

Because I couldn't smell my sister here any more than I had done in Jackal's underground hideout. Couldn't smell anything, actually, except the metallic bite of baking soda that matched the trail of human-shaped footprints following the path I'd just taken from stairwell to door.

Then, behind me, the trickle of a melody. Not a whistle this time, but the actual tinkle of Mama's music box emerging from the stairs I'd just walked up.

The killer was here, in my apartment building. And not bothering to think through the fact that, even in my frazzled state, I wouldn't have overlooked someone standing in the stairwell, I sprinted back in the direction from which I'd come. Thundered down the stairs so loudly residents pounded on their walls and swore at being woken. Pushed through the heavy fire door at the front entrance...and peered out into a seemingly empty street.

There was no one there. No one to match the trail of baking-soda footprints that disappeared as soon as it hit uneven pavement. No scent of shifter, no sound of music box, no magic tugging at my star ball and leading me toward the sister who should have been safely snuggled in her bed upstairs.

So, shoulders slumping, I looked in both directions one last time then climbed back up the stairs far more quietly than I'd rushed down them. And as I did so, I paid attention this time to the footprints, measuring their length in my mind's eye. The tracks were larger than my own feet but not so large they were definitively male...nor so small they were definitively female. The tread screamed athletic shoes but the stride was shorter than my own, suggesting whoever wore those sneakers didn't often use their gear to work out.

Which meant my visitor could have been about 80% of the people in the city. Good luck using that evidence to make an arrest.

Refusing to be disheartened by the lack of information, I made a beeline for my apartment as soon as I stepped out onto the third floor once again. The note was still there, the words gradually materializing as I puzzled out the pointy handwriting that had initially resembled nothing more than bird tracks in the snow.

And as I read, I gradually sank forward until my forehead rested on the scuffed surface of the door frame. Because the message was worse than expected, nothing like the overt threat Jackal would have offered. Instead, the words were polite, cultured...and marked the death knell of the secrecy that had protected me and my sister for the last twenty-five years.

"The artifacts aren't working as advertised," the note-writer informed me. *"The young fox is not an adequate guide. Come to the South Street bridge at midnight to renegotiate. Don't make this poor child suffer by bringing werewolves along."*

Chapter 25

I unlocked my door like an automaton, leaving it hanging open behind me as I headed into the kitchen in a daze. *It's happening.* The exposure I'd guarded against for decades hovered over my head like a storm cloud.

Good thing I'd gathered everything necessary to guard against the impending rain.

So I didn't enter Kira's bedroom to rail against her absence or take a much-needed shower. Instead, I climbed atop a wobbly kitchen chair and rooted around in the back of the cupboard for several long minutes, seeking the coffee neither Kira nor I drank.

Ah, there it was. Pre-ground crystals, still aromatic within their unsealed container. Pouring out the entire mess into the sink, I snatched up the ziplock bag of fake IDs that was revealed as the coffee grounds flowed out.

"Am I interrupting something?"

Good thing I was a fox or I would have fallen flat on my face when the lanky social worker waltzed through my door without bothering to knock first. As it was, the ziplock bag slid from suddenly nerveless fingers and I had to use a tendril of my star ball to nab the slippery plastic before it fluttered toward the floor.

Still, my voice was serene as I denied the truth to Simon's face. "Of course not. Just making coffee. Want some?"

As I spoke, I jumped down off the chair just a little too lightly to appear human...then made up for that lapse by scraping the wooden legs loudly across the floor while tucking the article of furniture back into its usual spot. I could almost hear Mr. Grouchy downstairs growling into his comforter, wanting to know why I couldn't keep banker's hours like everyone else...which might have explained why Simon was here. Had an ornery neighbor called Social Services just because I'd been too loud after dark?

I wasn't given time to pursue that supposition, though, because Simon responded with an easy "Sure," catching me off guard as he called my hospitality bluff for the very first time. What, now he wanted coffee? After years of politely evading my offers of tea and cookies? Of lifting his hands off the table when he accidentally brushed the surface, as if my bad housekeeping would rub off at a touch?

Unfortunately, while the sink was full of coffee crystals, the apartment possessed no brewing apparatus. And I wasn't even sure we still had a mug after Kira's most recent juggling attempt.

So I utilized one of my favorite game plans—when in doubt, go on the offensive. "What are you really here for?" I demanded, realizing as I spoke that there was no need to toady up to this social worker any longer regardless of his current reason for invading my home. Because, sure, for the last decade Simon had held the key to my happiness in his clammy fists. But Kira and I would shortly be starting over in a new community...and this time her ID would say she was over eighteen.

"To see your sister," the social worker replied, then proceeded to drawl out more explanation than he really needed. "I realized Kira wasn't here last time I spoke with you. Doesn't look like she's here now. Where is your ward?"

As he spoke, the male's eyes trailed across the combined kitchen and living room. And as Simon searched for a girl who was very obviously not present, my brain caught up with the adrenaline that had been coursing through my veins ever since the social worker barged in.

Wasn't his current behavior a little beyond the pale, even if the neighbors had called to report me? Since when did city workers make house calls late on a Friday evening? And why was he suddenly so intent upon seeing Kira?

My gut told me to get out of there, the sooner the better. And I trusted my gut. So I pasted on a smile and lied between my teeth.

"At a sleepover with a friend," I answered, mentally shuffling through the contents of the apartment as I spoke. Was there anything else Kira and I couldn't live without? Not really. My sister had sold Mama's last possessions, I kept all of our cash in my pockets, and our mother's star ball had recently been hanging out on my sister's person. Everything else was just so much jetsam ready to be thrown overboard as we abandoned ship.

"I'll go see her there then," Simon answered, breaking into my musings and accepting the deflection more easily than I'd expected. "What's the address?"

I was tempted to rattle off a fake street number then push the human out the door. But instinct told me he wasn't going to leave so easily. Might call in a coworker to check out my sto ry while he kept me talking, wasting time I could use to get my sister back.

So I parried rather than feinting. "Give me a minute. I'll hunt it down for you," I offered before slipping into the bedroom and closing the door in his face.

Then, just as I'd done two nights earlier, I gave into my fox's urge to flee the premises. It was ten times easier to do so in Kira's bedroom than it had been in that gas-station restroom, the window here a little larger and the fire escape on the outside providing an easy pathway to the ground.

"Hey! Wait!" Simon's face appeared at the window sooner than anticipated. But I didn't pause or answer, knowing his long arms and legs would take far too long to slip through the small gap after me. Instead, I just ran down the metal steps with heavy footfalls that once again wakened the neighbors. Then, knowing I was irredeemably cutting off all possibility of retreat, I slunk into the shadows and disappeared into the night.

Chapter 26

Unfortunately, I'd traversed only half a block when the scent of werewolf rose up around me. "Going somewhere?" Gunner demanded as he stepped out of an alcove to block my path.

I flinched backwards, wishing I could pretend I was still the same person I'd been one hour earlier. Then, I'd been glad for this male to join me. Yes, he was trouble. But he also seemed to possess a gentlemanly willingness to set aside my secrets in an effort to bring Kira back.

Now, though, my cards were face up on the table and I couldn't afford dragging an alpha werewolf along for the ride. So I hesitated one second longer than I should have...at which point Gunner struck.

Between one eye blink and the next, his hand was inside my pocket. Then the ziplock of fake IDs emerged squeezed between skillful fingers despite my attempt to twist away. "I..." I started...only to freeze as his other arm landed like a manacle around my waist while the first pried open the plastic bag.

"You're running," the alpha growled, his breath hot against the top of my head. He paged through paper and plastic that Kira and I would need to create a new life together, his voice turning chillier with each flipped over item. "Is your sister even missing? Or is that just another lie?"

"I've never lied to you," I countered, contemplating ways to free myself from my captor's handhold. Despite our size difference, I could have used his ill-considered grip to throw Gunner over my back so I could flee while he lay winded on the pavement. Or my star-ball-turned-dagger could stab the pesky werewolf in the gut for a more final form of freedom than that.

And yet I hovered indecisively, kicking myself for being unwilling to make a move against Gunner. My Arena fights had gone south many times over the last decade, with dozens of matches ending in hospitalizations rather than a simple scratch on the cheek. So why did the mere thought of injuring a werewolf make me shiver uncontrollably now?

No matter the reason, my opponent didn't miss the change in mood. His arm softened as he pulled me in closer, and his next words were midway between human speech and werewolf growl. "Tell me what's wrong and I'll fix it," the male murmured.

He sounded so solid, so dependable. But before I could answer, the decision was taken out of my hands. First came a yip followed by a single howl...then the cacophony grew until lupine voices were erupting all around us from over a dozen throats.

The newcomers must have scouted the scene before announcing themselves, because they weren't coming from one direction alone. Instead, they'd blocked passage down the street in both directions, north and south pathways equally cut off from the potential for retreat.

I spared one quick glance toward the alpha who still held me up against him, hoping this was merely Atwood backup finally making themselves known. But, of course, Gunner would never have allowed such overt wolfishness in a human neighborhood. So I wasn't at all surprised to see the alpha's eyebrow's rising while the air around us filled with the unmistakable tang of fur.

Nope, the encroaching pack wasn't friendly. And, based on their numbers, Gunner and I were dramatically outmatched.

"PUT THIS SOMEWHERE safe, then shift."

The ziplock of IDs whizzed toward me even as Gunner spun away to peer down the darkened street in both directions. And while I *did* take the time to carefully stash the bag into an inside pocket, I just as overtly disobeyed the alpha's second command. After all, donning my fox form would have been sure suicide. So I molded my star ball into a sword instead and came to stand beside Gunner on two human feet.

"You'd be safer as a wolf," he observed, although I noticed the male made no move to follow his own advice. Then, when I didn't answer: "I don't suppose you have another sword I could borrow?"

"Here." I hoped the darkness was deep enough so my companion couldn't·see my rapier narrowing by half as I pulled a second weapon out of the sheathe along my spine. Star-ball metal was strong if formed properly, so I wasn't worried that even a half-width blade might fail to do its job.

What was more concerning was whether being separated from so much of my magic would dull my reaction time. Strangely, I felt stronger rather than weaker as the not-quite-solid weapon slipped into my companion's waiting hand.

Gunner nodded his thanks briefly before calling out into the darkness as the click of nails on pavement grew audible against the night. "Last chance to talk out our differences. Don't start something you're going to regret."

It was a nice gesture on his part, but none of the enemy shifters currently possessed human vocal cords with which to reply to him. Nor did they have any interest in backing down. Instead, they sprang upon us in two synchronized waves, yips and snarls preceding fur and claws by barely enough seconds to allow me to angle my sword toward the shadows rushing toward me out of the night.

After that, nothing but fangs and growls mattered. And I had to admit that even my star ball wouldn't have been enough to keep me afloat had I been flying solo. But, back to back with Gunner, we were able to fend off the attackers even if we failed to gain actual ground.

The night was dark and the wolves were many, so it took me quite a while to figure out who we were fighting against. *Jackal*, I realized, picking out the white-ruffed wolf even as I sliced a wicked wound through the hamstring of his second in command. Had I been wrong in my reassessing of the situation? Was my pretend boyfriend the strangely polite note-leaver who had snatched my sister off the street in pursuit of an agenda of his own?

As if sensing my confusion, Jackal shimmered upward into humanity even as two of his pack mates attempted to take me down from the left and right. Good thing Gunner had eyes in the back of his head...or at least the alpha fought as if he did. Knocking one wolf onto its tail with a rather impressive side kick, my partner opened up enough space so I could swipe a welt across the other wolf's nose.

Then Jackal was standing naked in the middle of the street without concern for shifter secrecy or human modesty. "You made the wrong decision, little girl," he told me, advancing forward until he stood just beyond the reach of my sword. "I would have protected you. This filth will not."

In reaction, Gunner growled deep in his throat, his back muscles tightening where they pressed up against my own. But my companion didn't turn his head to answer, just kept attacking and parrying while providing leeway in which I could speak.

"I want my sister back," I demanded, ignoring Jackal's insults and cutting straight to the heart of the matter. "What is it you want in exchange?"

And to my surprise, my opponent's brow furrowed while his head tilted to one side. "You want your sister *back*?"

I had just enough time to realize Jackal had no idea what I was talking about—that he hadn't been the kidnapper and note-writer and presumably had no notion that I shifted into the form of a fox rather than that of a wolf. But before I could decide how that understanding changed the face of the current battle, Gunner roared behind me...and a strange lethargy flooded my limbs.

Meanwhile, a gleaming *something* whizzed away into the darkness even as my legs began trembling with their effort to hold me erect. I whimpered like a puppy, my vision turned muddy, then—to my eternal chagrin—I fell onto my knees.

Chapter 27

I was vaguely aware of an unpadded shoulder cutting into my belly as blood rushed to my upside-down head. Then I was lying flat on my back atop a foul-smelling dumpster, Gunner's hands rubbing heat back into my limbs.

"Damn it, wake up!"

I wasn't unconscious and I tried to tell him as much. But the attempted words instead came out as a moan even as the scent of fur dampened into bitter-almond concern.

Gunner dropped his sword, I realized, the words materializing far more slowly than they should have as my own star-ball-turned-weapon throbbed in my clenched right fist. Which explained why I was suddenly weak as a newborn kitten, unable to do more than roll over onto my side and strain against the darkness in search of the other half of my soul.

To my relief, the second sword hadn't entirely disappeared into the night. Instead, it was clearly visible twenty feet distant, lying at the feet of a snarling werewolf. If I could just....

Before I could muster sufficient energy to do anything, though, Gunner was tilting my torso upright and piercing me with the intensity of his gaze. "Mai, talk to me."

He sounded so desperately worried. And even though I knew I had more important matters to contend with, I succumbed to the fuzzy need within my belly. Raised my left hand. Trailed two fingers along the knife edge of his jaw...

...then jerked aside as skin-on-skin contact hit me like an electric shock. Even the mud in my brain settled in that moment. And this time when I yanked at the distant sword with all of my remaining vigor, the weapon gradually dislodged itself from the ground and began dragging itself toward my wiggling fingers.

Meanwhile, I did my best to stem Gunner's angst by letting him know I wasn't actually perishing at his feet. "I'm fine," I told him...the words coming out more like "I fie." Unfortunately, from the whiteness surrounding the alpha's lips, my consolation hadn't hit its intended mark.

But I'd be able to mollify my companion with fully-formed words sooner rather than later. Because the sword was arcing up toward us now, slicing through the ear of a werewolf who had been attempting to scramble up the sheer side of the dumpster protecting us from the melee below. The four-legger yelped and Gunner whirled...and I did the only thing I could think of to prevent my companion from seeing a sword break the laws of physics as it flew upward toward our perch.

I allowed the weapon in my right hand to dissolve into starlight then used those freed digits to pull my companion's head down toward me. After that, I kissed him, our lips merging together even as metal-turned-magic reunited with my grasping left hand.

Hot and sweet and rough all at once, enchantment and sensation exploded inside me in a jumbled mixture that could have been pure passion or might have just been the energetic reunion with my star-ball-turned-sword.

Either way, I didn't have long to ponder the issue. Because Jackal was no dummy and his henchmen had access to human fingers if they chose them. So it didn't take long for several two-leggers to build a ramp of debris leading to our aerial retreat while others maintained their four-legged forms to serve as the vanguard. Now, muzzles mounted the dumpster, hot breath sneaking down the top of my boots while blood-crazed eyes glowed against the night.

"Shift!" I ordered Gunner, breaking our connection as quickly as it had begun and pushing backwards out of his arms. For half a second he continued to hold me. But then the alpha's eyes cleared and sharpened as the air filled with incipient fur.

Gunner must have assumed I intended to join him in four-legged battle. Because he didn't spare me a second glance, just dropped down into the form of his wolf, fragments of shredded clothing spraying out around him. And while I would have liked to once again stand back to back with the alpha and fend off Jackal's underlings, our kiss had re-awoken the count-down timer inside my head.

If Jackal wasn't the kidnapper, then someone else was out there threatening the life of my sister. And that someone had left me a very small window in which to reach the South Street bridge.

There was no world in which I chose to ignore the mandated meeting. And, given the contents of that note, it was safer to do so without being trailed by even a friendly wolf. So as Jackal's army leapt up onto the dumpster one after another, I backed away rather than raising my sword and diving into battle. Gunner growled at the intruders, protecting me with his body...and I took advantage of his lapse of attention to slide through the cracked window behind us and leave my overprotective companion-at-arms behind.

I WAS USED TO TRAVERSING the city in solitude. So why did I suddenly feel so queasy as I left the alpha to fight off a dozen werewolves with nothing but his claws and teeth?

"Gunner can take care of himself," I muttered under my breath, guilt dogging my footsteps as I ran down graffitied steps and entered the nearest subway station. I'd evaded Pickle Breath and three of his cronies along the way, the teenager's presence suggesting he'd been dogging my footsteps earlier as a paid lackey of the werewolf I'd recently fought against. But neither shifter nor human would be able to follow after metal wheels and the press of humanity eradicated my trail.

I pulled out bills to feed the fare machine...then inhaled sharply as I realized what I held within my hand. Ma Scrubbs' doorman hadn't presented me with a big wad of twenties this afternoon the way I'd expected. No, these were hundred-dollar bills, far more than I would have expected to rake in over the course of a month, let alone from a single night's work.

I hesitated, but a far-too-close howl returned me to my senses. There was a train incoming and I needed to be through those doors before anyone caught up and followed on my heels....

So I pushed the bills deeper into my pocket, zipped the closure, then rushed through the turnstile at a sprint. And twenty minutes and two transfers later, I was emerging from the underground maze with the breeze off the river ruffling through my hair.

I'd made it. Ten minutes early even, the brightly lit bridge arching over water that flowed endlessly underneath. And sure, I lacked a game plan. But I trusted my fox senses and my star ball to get me out of any pinch.

Plus, there was always the Arena windfall to consider. Maybe Kira's kidnapper would be willing to trade my sister for cold, hard cash?

Padding away from my destination rather than toward it, I took in the bridge a second time out of the corner of one eye. The kidnapper would have arrived hours earlier, I suspected, both to scout the area and to ensure I didn't appear at the head of an army of werewolves. So I wasn't surprised when flickers of movement materialized into dark-coated figures scattered hither and yon across the open expanse...wasn't surprised but was prompted toward deeper stealth.

There were half a dozen of the watchers. One pretended to read a newspaper on a bench by the bus stop, one walked a dog down the sidewalk, and two lingered on nearby rooftops.

It was the sixth waiting figure, however, who gave me the clue that my initial read of the situation had been dramatically off kilter. His sedan idled down by the river, the glow of a cigarette lighting his stubbled face. The male looked like any hardened criminal, but his car was too blocky and well-maintained to mesh with that disguise....

I took a step back, adrenaline flooding my bloodstream. Because while I'd thought I was walking into one kind of trap, it appeared I had instead nearly stumbled into another.

These men weren't aligned with Kira's kidnapper. No, these figures keeping eyes peeled for newcomers were instead entirely human. They were city cops.

Chapter 28

It was one of the hardest things I'd ever done, but I turned on my heel and walked away from the only clue I possessed pertaining to my sister's current location. I maintained a disingenuous saunter until I rounded the corner, then I broke into a slightly superhuman run.

The note on the door. I saw the small, white square in my mind's eye as vividly as if I was actually standing on the well-worn carpet in the apartment building's third-floor hallway. I'd read the kidnapper's missive, had hurried inside to hunt down forged identification documents...then had forgotten all about the scrap of paper when Simon's presence sent me scurrying down the fire escape to beat my retreat.

Of course Kira's pesky social worker would have found the note. His broad shoulders had no chance of fitting through that window, which meant Simon would have left via the more traditional route. When he closed the door, the square of paper would have been staring him in the face, adding mentions of werewolves and artifacts to my earlier evasions about Kira's current whereabouts. No wonder he'd contacted the police department and set up an amber alert, then sent out a net of officials to scoop me up.

It all made perfect sense...and, unfortunately, turned Kira's future even murkier than it had been before. Because human authority figures sniffing around my trail meant that the one open channel of communication between myself and my sister's kidnappers had just slammed shut in my face.

Inhaling deeply through my nostrils, I reminded myself that I wasn't entirely out of resources just yet. The city was dark but far from sleeping as I angled my way into the red-light district, planning to hit up acquaintances who kept their ear trained to the street. Unfortunately, a string of prostitutes and black-market thiefspawns slammed their doors in my face one after another. And at the end of the block, the fear widening Joe Sly's face as soon as I entered his establishment suggested my usual resources had a more unified reason to clam up.

"Just let anyone who's interested know that I'm willing to negotiate," I told the bartender rather than bothering with a question he was clearly unwilling to answer. "I won't be reachable through the usual channels. But they *can* call me on this cell." I rattled off the numbers of a newly bought burner phone then waited impatiently as Joe failed to write even a single digit down.

"I don't know who I'd give this to," the vertically challenged old-timer muttered, glowering up at me from beneath bushy brows. He was lying through his teeth, I noted...which confused the issue further. After all, as best I could tell, Joe was entirely human and didn't have a clue about shifters' existence. If it wasn't sharp-toothed werewolves putting the fear of death into him, then what sort of terror would keep this leathery survivor from even passing along a measly note?

Kira's round face rose in my mind, and this time I succumbed to the urge to beg. "Please," I said. "I'm hunting for my sister...."

Joe gave me the fish eye, but the male *did* eventually write down my digits. Still, I had a sinking suspicion he was going to ditch the napkin as soon as I turned my back.

The pulsing neon lights strobed behind me as I stepped outside, tucking my chin deeper into my coat. It was turning colder by the minute, so I wasn't entirely surprised to feel the soft chill of snow landing atop my cheekbones as I turned my face up toward the sky.

"Now would be a good time for vague hints, Mama," I whispered starward, figuring the drunken teenagers behind my back were too engrossed in whooping it up to notice I was speaking to nobody but myself. Unfortunately, I really did seem to be talking to snowflakes only. Because no answers were forthcoming even from inside my own head.

I WANDERED FOR HOURS after that until the first glint of dawn overcame the glow of half-strength streetlights. A businessman had offered to pay me for sex, two frat boys had made an even less successful attempt at pushing me to the pavement, and I'd been roundly ignored by all permanent residents of my home turf. All told, I was exhausted, frustrated...and scared to death that Kira's kidnapper would harm my sister due to circumstances beyond my ability to control.

"Don't make this poor child suffer..." The polished nature of the written words didn't lower their threat value one iota, and I shivered as I remembered the homeless guy hidden beneath the bridge with the imprint of Mama's medallion frozen into his chest. That could be Kira if I didn't find her quickly....

But I'd twisted metaphorical arms all night, and now my contact information was almost certainly flowing down the grapevine between myself and whoever held my sister hostage. Which meant I might as well take cover and ensure no nosy cops found me while I waited for the kidnapper to call.

To that end, I ducked into a dank public bathroom, tucking clothes and personal belongings into a star-ball-created yoke around my stomach before donning the body of my fox. Nosing out from under the stall door in red-furred splendor, it was easy to hop up onto the sink then slither out the broken window placed just underneath the eaves.

For half a second, I teetered there atop the chipped concrete, breathing in the freedom of becoming a fox. Snow was falling harder now, the white blanket covering up grime and making the city appear both clean and new. And I couldn't help thinking how much Kira would have loved the snow storm, how her eyes would sparkle while her cheeks turned pleasure-pink.

Today, though, Kira would enjoy neither snowmen nor hot chocolate. Instead, she was caught in the grasp of a shadowy force dark enough to make even Joe Sly run scared. No wonder focusing on my sister resulted in a sharp pain within my gut.

But...wait...was that ache merely remorseful wallowing? Or was something else going on?

Because between one gust of snow-laden wind and the next, the burn had gained a direction that tugged my vulpine feet forward. Merely swiveling my body to face north lessened the agony momentarily. And when I hopped to the ground and took one tentative step in that direction, my stomach warmed and the pain lessened...only to bubble back to burning agony when I planted my furry feet rather than continuing along the indicated route.

It was never a good idea to get caught up in unknown magic. But I'd been wandering aimlessly for hours and was glad to be pulled in any direction, even a bad one. So I didn't try to resist the tug further. Instead, I sprinted north out of the Warrens, twisting and turning down curvy alleys guided by the compass within my stomach.

I stopped only once to bite ice balls out from between my paw pads. The snow was growing deeper now and the day had warmed just enough for the heat of my skin to melt fluff into ice. But my muscles tensed and I barely managed to pause long enough to catch my breath before the tug in my gut yanked me forward. And I somehow wasn't surprised when Mama's voice sprang to life with yet another warning I couldn't puzzle out.

"Hang out a sheep head to sell dog meat," my mother's voice noted. And as I panted, pressed against the side of a building, I realized I knew exactly where I was for the first time in over an hour.

The nearby houses had turned huge several moments earlier, but my tired brain hadn't made the obvious connection until I recognized the cavalcade of parked cars half-covered by blankets of white. In my defense, snow stifled scents and blowing particles obstructed vision, so it was hard to tell I was walking directly into danger until werewolves rose out of the white haze before me while the overwhelming scent of Atwood finally filtered into my nose.

So that's what Mama meant. Walking up to the ruling werewolf's den in the body of a fox was a recipe for disaster, and I could only hope it wasn't already too late to hide whatever secrets I had left. So I pushed upwards into humanity then shivered as bare feet froze upon contact with an ankle-deep layer of snow and ice.

Chapter 29

"Tank, Allen, Crow," I greeted the trio, tension melting off my shoulders as I took in the identities of the males emerging out of the swirling snow. Unfortunately, my relief was short-lived because none of Gunner's pack mates returned the greeting. Instead, Tank and Crow shifted into fur form without bothering to remove their clothing first, while Allen lunged sideways on human feet to cut off my easiest avenue of escape.

They know what I am. To my eternal chagrin, I neither fled nor attacked in the face of this culmination of my recurring nightmare. Instead, I stood there, naked save for the not-quite-fanny-pack around my waist, trying to decide whether I could get away with yanking a sword out of the ether without sealing Kira's fate as well as my own.

After all, it was still possible the trio hadn't noted my white-tipped tail and vulpine whiskers when they first came upon me in the snow....

While I hesitated, the pack's accountant cleared the air. "The boss was disappointed you ran off and left him," Allen informed me, his words a rough growl backed up by the hard knock of his shoulder against my own. And maybe the night spent scouring the city in search of my sister had exhausted me more than I realized, or maybe I was just shocked by the bitter violence emanating from a once-gentle shifter. Whatever the reason, Allen's blow threw me off balance...then a wolf to the back of my knees sent me toppling over into a drift of snow.

Frozen water crystals molded around my body like a not-so-warm trenchcoat. But it was the increasing pain within my gut that left me doubled over...that plus a realization of why I'd been drawn to this mansion in the first place.

My debt to Gunner. Of course. I owed the alpha three bucks plus interest. And whether he'd called in the tab intentionally or by accident, I still found myself crawling away from my attackers and toward the building's rear entrance rather than saving my skin by beating a hasty retreat.

Unfortunately, the werewolves around me must have thought I was trying to flee rather than accepting my comeuppance. Because snarls tunneled through the snow clogging my ear canals, then wolf teeth scraped against the naked skin of my calf.

In response, my star ball pulsed against frozen fingers. The magic wasn't subtle enough to understand the consequences of forming armored long johns or spiked garters when I was currently buck naked. Instead, it pushed me to provide guidance. Should we attack or defend?

"Neither," I began, the stab of agony spreading from my belly into my temples making it nearly impossible to speak. But the word didn't entirely materialize since my cheek was now pressed against a snow drift. Instead, I coughed as I inhaled a mouthful of solid snow.

I lay there spluttering, unable to twist aside as a second wolf pounced upon what little bit of my face was currently accessible. Foul breath wafted into my nostrils even as the wound in my leg deepened sufficiently to impinge upon the pounding in my head and gut. These weren't the same cheerful pack mates who had ferried me around the city yesterday. Instead, I was facing angry werewolves out for enemy blood....

Which is when I lost track of self-preservation and let instinct take over. Yanking at my fox nature in terror, I prepared to disengage and flee in my agile vulpine form.

But my shift was blocked by the debt dragging me toward the now invisible mansion, and I wasn't able to so much as twist out of the duo's tightening grasp.

"I'm sorry, Kira," I murmured as I stopped straining against the impossible. It was finally time to admit defeat.

"LET HER UP."

Gunner's command would have been more welcome if his tone hadn't been as cold as the snow packed between my butt cheeks. So it wasn't terribly surprising that his underlings obeyed the spirit rather than the actual letter of his order. Tank and Crow *did* let me go long enough to regain their own humanity, but Allen took advantage of the lull to haul me up by my hair. Then naked two-leggers regained the holds recently relinquished by lupine jaws, this time grabbing my arms in a vise-like grip that was no more yielding than their teeth had been.

Meanwhile, the snowfall was easing up around us, which made it easier than it would have been previously to see the tall male figure stalking down the mansion's rear path toward our circle of trampled snow. And I cringed as I took in the bandage crossing Gunner's cheekbone, the bruises around his throat, and the way the alpha walked with an ill-disguised limp.

The odds *had* been badly stacked against him back by my apartment, especially after I'd abandoned the male to duke it out alone. Gunner was lucky he'd made it out of that dog pile alive, and his current existence was no thanks to me.

"I'm sorry," I started...only to lose track of apologies as the phone in my fanny pack buzzed angrily against my belly. Of all the moments for my trails of bread crumbs to finally bear fruit, now was *not* the time for Kira's kidnapper to call.

Unfortunately, the hands gripping my arms only bit in tighter as I attempted to reach for the potential lifeline. And there was no warmth in Gunner's eyes as he watched me struggle in silence for one long second before I accepted the futility of the attempt.

"Someone more important you need to talk to?" the alpha asked as I stilled, proving that his shifter ears made him well aware of the call that would soon be shunted over to voice mail. He stalked one step closer until I was sandwiched between so many male bodies my breath caught within my throat. And, despite everything, my skin still tingled as the alpha's warm breath blew miniature tornadoes through my ice-streaked hair.

"I was wrong about Jackal," I answered as quickly as I could while trying to remember how many times the phone had buzzed at me already. Three, four? Would Kira's kidnapper try again if I didn't pick up, or would this be my second strike that knocked my sister's rescue off the table for good? "This call is..."

I didn't even manage to get out the rest of my sentence before Gunner reached toward my belly, feeling for the zipper that didn't actually exist. *Open,* I bade the star ball, and the alpha's scent sharpened as the cell jumped out into his extended hand.

Then the screen was glowing between us, *"Unknown name, unknown number"* filling the small rectangle. I stretched toward it even though I knew Tank and Crow wouldn't release me. And secretiveness or no secretiveness, if I'd been able I would have pressed the appropriate button with the power of my mind.

Unfortunately, I wasn't that powerful. And the alpha before me didn't appear ready to soften his stance anytime soon either. "If you want to answer, you'll promise to stop running," Gunner growled, still up in my face.

The air between us was so full of fur and electricity that I nearly choked on my next inhale. Still, I managed to nod. And when Gunner raised his eyebrows, clearly requiring verbal confirmation, I breathed out a vow that dug debt-bearing claws yet deeper into my gut. "I promise."

At which point the fingers holding back my right arm loosened, allowing me to snatch the cell phone out of my companion's extended hand. I slid damp fingers across the slick surface, relieved when the call picked up. Then I turned my back for the barest illusion of privacy while pressing the cold plastic up against my ear. "Yes?" I answered, the single word all I could muster using long pent-up air.

"You've just about blown it." Ma Scrubbs' creaky old voice was the last one I'd expected to wend its way out of the speaker. But as she continued, the entire charade suddenly made far too much sense. "I've turned Kira over to the client," the old woman who loved money above all else informed me, "so you'd better turn up fast."

Chapter 30

"**M**a, don't do it!"

"I've told you before that I'm not your mother." I could imagine the old woman puffing herself up the way she used to when I trailed into the Arena on my father's heels, a lanky teenager with dreams even larger than my sword. Ma Scrubbs had doled out tough love then, but there was no affection mixed into the harshness of her voice when she continued now. "I'm looking out for number one. About damn time you did the same."

Then the cell phone was no longer pressed up against my chilled cartilage. Gunner had snatched the device away, transferring the call over to speaker phone in the process. "Where is Kira?" he demanded.

My companion's words were so full of alpha electricity that they would have easily compelled a werewolf to reply. But Ma Scrubbs merely laughed. "Hey there, boy scout. Whatcha gonna offer me in exchange?"

"What do you want?" I couldn't believe it, but Gunner was negotiating with the woman. Was apparently willing to offer any of his rather astonishingly large array of assets in exchange for my sister's life. Within my belly, the milk-money debt grew into a dragon...and I willingly allowed its foothold to increase.

Ma Scrubbs, unfortunately, was less impressed by the offer. "Naw, naw, I got what I wanted. The client's funding my retirement. I'm off to the Caribbean. Or maybe the Mediterranean. Never could keep those warm-water oceans straight...."

"Ma!" I couldn't help myself. Because Kira was in the hands of someone who'd used kitsune magic to murder at least two people recently. Given the obvious danger of that situation, Ma Scrubbs couldn't just offer a vague warning then hang up on me....

Unfortunately, the only response I came up with beyond her name was a strangled growl. So it was probably a good thing Gunner continued his negotiations without any loss of steam. "But think of how nice it would be to live in a mansion rather than in a straw hut during your golden years. Give me a routing number and I'll transfer over a million bucks. All you have to do is tell me where Kira is right now."

"Money first," Ma countered. "And you'd better hurry. The client is already on his way to pick her up."

Nails bit into my palms, but I forced myself to remain silent. I wasn't helping matters by emoting. Somehow the werewolf beside me was able to able to speak the old woman's language better than I could, so I might as well let him continue blazing the path.

"You give me an address and we'll transfer funds during the drive over," Gunner replied smoothly, proving my point even as he began pushing me toward one of the waiting vehicles. Without requiring nudges of their own, the alpha's three underlings slid into seats while pulling on clothes soppy with melted snow. Tank and Crow got in the front, Allen aimed for the third tier, and the middle row sat open and waiting to thaw my frozen skin.

But rather than joining the other werewolves inside the steaming vehicle, I found myself shifting from foot to foot in ankle-deep snow while Gunner completed the deal-making aspect of the morning. "I'm a boy scout, remember. You know I'll keep my word," the alpha growled when Ma Scrubbs' silence proved her unwillingness to pony up before she was paid.

"Better hold him to that, girlie," Ma said after one last moment of endless consideration. And I could hear in her voice that she, at least, understood the secrets I didn't want revealed.

"Yes," I answered, voice catching in a way that caused all four werewolves to eye me oddly. But then Ma Scrubbs was rattling off an address that was far too familiar, giving me something new to worry about.

Because the old woman hadn't stashed Kira anywhere easy to access. Instead, she'd stuck my sister in the Warren, where Jackal's riled-up wolves ruled the roost.

THERE WERE SO MANY zeros on the screen of Allen's cell phone that I gulped. Still, I'd accepted the debt already. So I busied myself pulling my leather jacket out of the star-ball-turned-fanny-pack, hoping no one noticed that the space was far too small to contain such a bulky object without the assistance of magic. Meanwhile, I promised aloud what my kitsune nature required as recompense to the alpha pressed far too close against my side. "I'll pay you back."

Was I just imagining the faint smile quirking up the corner of Gunner's lips as the debt within my belly ballooned from draconic to sea-monster size? Probably. Because all he said was: "Let's worry about that later." Then his eyes widened as they returned to the road.

"*Stop*," he ordered, his alpha command causing the male behind the wheel to slam on the brakes before easing up his foot and pulling into an empty parking space.

"Boss?" Allen asked from behind us, leaning over the seats to peer over his alpha's shoulder. "I thought we were in a hurry...."

"Cops," Gunner noted succinctly. And now that he mentioned it, I *could* just barely make out the taillights of stalled traffic three blocks ahead. Still, the leap from there to a police barricade...wasn't really that great once I remembered that every policeman in the city was likely staring at pictures of Kira's and my faces at the present moment. A fact Gunner now knew as well as I did since I'd clued him in to all relevant details during the five minutes we'd spent on the road.

"*The weak are meat. The strong eat*," my mother murmured inside my head. And even though I only narrowed my eyes slightly, I was pretty sure Gunner didn't miss the fact that I'd just been graced with another missive from my maternal spirit. Instead, his eyes bored into mine like icicles. And despite the heat blowing out of the vent above my head, I felt very much as if I was back outside, standing naked in the snow.

Yes, I hadn't mentioned my kitsune nature or the dead-mother-voices-in-my-head during the hurried debrief. So sue me. At least I wasn't actively running away.

"We can park here and get there easily as wolves," Tank noted when no one else suggested a game plan. "The destination is only four blocks away."

For a werewolf, the idea was a good one. But for a kitsune.... I needed to arrive two-legged if there was to be a single sliver of hope that Kira and I might survive our upcoming meeting with skins intact.

So I pushed open the car door without speaking, preparing to make tracks away from the werewolf who represented both my greatest asset and my greatest weakness wrapped up together in one overbearing package. I had no plan. Just an instinctive urge to reach my sister before anyone could threaten her further.

But I wasn't actually able to force a single foot outside the vehicle. My debt was holding me far too strongly within its grip.

"No, we'll walk there two-legged," Gunner decided after what felt like an eternity. "Crow, you take point. Allen and Tank bring up the rear. Whatever happens, your top priority is to protect Kira and Mai."

Chapter 31

Something about Gunner's command unstuck my feet and allowed me to slip out of the SUV without waiting for my companions to follow. But electricity pulsing against my skin promised werewolves were fast on my heels as I turned into the first of several alleys too narrow for a vehicle to traverse. I'd have little time to cover up any fox-related lapses before the quartet reached my sister's side....

And, in the end, Gunner's proximity turned out to be an asset rather than a hindrance. Because as I barreled around a corner without bothering to scout for danger, a growling werewolf stepped directly into my path. His distinctive scent of strawberries and asphalt was entirely unfamiliar, suggesting he wasn't one of the dozen or so shifters I'd smelled within Gunner's compound. Meanwhile, the greedy smile on his face suggested he had a very specific idea of what to do with me.

But whether the male was a new initiate into Jackal's army or merely a drifter with murder on his mind, I wasn't a lone fox any longer. Instead, pounding footsteps behind me soon turned into four angry shifters surrounding me in their midst. And before I could speak, Gunner reached out and smacked the strange male upside the head.

"What are you *doing*?" The strawberry-asphalt shifter sounded more surprised than angry, although Gunner's answer had enough rage embedded in his tone for both of their sakes.

"Preventing you from making a very unfortunate mistake," the alpha answered. Gunner's body seemed to double in size as he loomed over the other shifter, and—predictably—the weaker wolf cringed away from his alpha's disdain. "I told you to keep Ransom back home in safety. And the backup I requested was meant to block off the Warren's perimeter only. Why are you here rather than with him?"

"Chief Ransom decided..."

I didn't bother waiting for what seemed inclined to turn into a string of excuses. Because if this male was an Atwood werewolf, then I had no need to hang around and listen to the dressing down of a subordinate. Kira's life hung in the balance and I had more important places to be.

So I slunk sideways, unsurprised when Gunner's eyes flicked away from his underling to latch onto me. He didn't call me back, though. Just nodded at his men to stick to my heels as he finished his own task.

"The early one wins," Mama murmured as my feet once again slid silently over snow-lined pavement. And I didn't even flinch this time, just continued winding through the maze of alleys that stood between me and my ultimate goal.

Because I was beginning to guess where the twists and turns were leading me. Sure enough, moments later a grand old opera building rose mid-block, its slightly decaying edifice elegant against the snow. I didn't need to check the address to know this was where Ma Scrubbs had stashed my sister. Not when the derelict structure should have been empty...and yet a string of large footprints led up to and away from the front door.

An equal number of people appeared to have walked out as had initially entered, but I didn't take that assumption for fact. After all, I was frantic rather than stupid. And I was pretty sure I'd caught the scent of Pickle Breath a mere block distant, the teenage hoodlum's presence in the wrong place at the right moment suggesting Jackal wasn't far away.

I didn't want to draw attention to myself so close to where—I hoped—my sister waited. So instead of taking the direct approach, I slipped around the side, found an unlocked window, and shimmied my way through. My werewolf bodyguards swore beneath their breath, too large to follow. But I ignored their recriminations, tiptoeing out of the changing room without pause and heading down a narrow hall.

"*...shift for me and we'll call it even.*" The voice emerged as I neared the stage entrance. Robotic, uninflected, as if someone had used a computer to anonymize their existence. Meanwhile, I smelled my sister's terror...but caught nothing else beyond stale notes of long-absent beings filling the massive space.

My fox senses bade me to scout the surroundings further, to spend time figuring out what kind of trap waited for me atop the stage. But Kira gasped, and I didn't hesitate. Instead, I stepped out into the open...and saw the sister I'd sworn to protect dangling twenty feet above my head at the end of a rapidly fraying rope.

"KIRA, SHIFT!" I YELLED up at her, vaguely taking in the laptop lying near my feet. The screen was blank, the webcam pointed toward the ceiling. Someone had gone to a great deal of effort to capture the visual of a shifting kitsune...and yet that still appeared to be the only way for my sister to escape from the deteriorating harness that rucked up beneath her armpits.

"I can't," Kira moaned, her face so white it might as well have been coated with the snow still falling outside the theater. "I sold the star ball to Ma Scrubbs so we could pay our bills. I *trusted* her, so I followed her out of the park like an idiot when she came up to me today...." Kira caught her breath against a sob, straightened her spine, then returned to the matter at hand. "So I *can't* shift now," she informed me. "Not without Mama's star ball. I *could* untie the knot, but then I'd just *fall*...."

And now the entire messy endeavor finally made sense. *That* was what Ma Scrubbs had initially pawned off on the killer. *That* was what the shadowy being was trying to find a way to unleash—the true power of a kitsune's star ball. Magic that could move at least metaphorical mountains if placed in the wrong hands.

The repercussions of fox-shifter magic entering the mainstream were potentially earth-shattering, but I couldn't find it within my heart to care at the moment. Instead, I eyed the series of catwalks that would allow moderately easy access to the space near the ceiling. Ma Scrubbs' people must have used the elevated walkways to hook Kira onto the end of a fly-line in the first place. I could just follow their lead and reel my sister in using the reverse of their actions....

Or so I guessed in the split second I spent taking in the setup. Unfortunately, the rope my sister dangled from had been sawed three-quarters of the way through, and her weight now tested its limits. Even as I watched, yet another strand broke free.

"Mai!"

I'd been responding to my sister's distress cries since she was an infant. So I didn't need the tug on my gut to send me scurrying toward the ladder leading upward. My feet thundered across the first catwalk even as I was plotting my approach, and I turned left to angle closer...only to find twenty feet of open air gaping between myself and the suspended child.

Clever, Ma. The old woman's helpers had strung Kira up, then dismantled the most relevant part of the catwalk behind them. Of course they had. They wanted to ensure that the only way out of Kira's conundrum was to leap away in the body of a fox.

Which my sister couldn't do...but *I* could.

"Untie the knots," I told Kira, knowing as I spoke that she would make short work of even pulled-tight tangles. After all, replicating Houdini's coffin-in-the-river trick had been one of her favorite afternoon activities in lieu of homework...well, without the underwater part. I'd had to put my foot down somewhere.

Ignoring the urge to leap without looking, I gauged the distance even as I slipped out of my clothing piece by piece. I couldn't jump that far as a human, but it would be easy in vulpine form. Assuming Kira untied herself in the interim, my body slamming into hers should take us both to the catwalk on the other side. And, after that, we'd be home free....

"Look down!" my sister demanded one second before I tugged at my star ball and seized my animal form. My eyes flicked in the indicated direction, and I swore beneath my breath as I noted five faces peering up out of what had formerly been an entirely empty audience hall.

Gunner and his trio of pack mates stood just inside the main entrance as a unit...and if they'd been the only ones present I might have come out on the other side of my upcoming transformation alive. After all, my employer had proven himself thoughtful and trustworthy. Surely he'd understand that I wasn't evil merely because I'd been born allied with an inner fox.

So it was really the fifth face that pulled the breath out of me. Ransom. I recognized Gunner's brother from our fight at the Arena. Knew even though the distance was too great to pick out his features that the male's brow was lowered as he tried to understand what I meant to do.

Because a wolf couldn't make the leap from catwalk to child. Nor could a human. I'd only manage to save my sister if I took on the body of a fox.

Gunner might give me time to explain before tearing me to pieces. But his brother was a pack leader in charge of hundreds of werewolves. He'd toe the party line and sign my death warrant himself.

On the other hand, a nearly inaudible snap promised that Kira's rope was fraying rapidly. And she was suspended above a spine-shattering expanse of unyielding floorboards.

By my estimate, we had less than ten seconds to save her. So I shrugged off the future, ignored my audience...and, at long last, I found my fur.

Chapter 32

Foxes are world-class climbers and pretty good jumpers. But I wasn't just a fox. I was kitsune—ten times better than that.

So my muscles vibrated with tension as I ignored the chatter beneath me. I breathed into my stomach as Dad had taught me. Then I pushed off, nails snagging on gridded metal as I launched myself into the air.

Wind rushed past my fur and my sister giggled in delight before me. She could feel the buzz of woken star ball expanding my lungs, could sense the pure freedom that filled my heart as I embraced the form I was meant to wear.

I was a fox for five short seconds only. Had rebuilt myself into a naked woman even before slamming into a blessedly unhindered Kira. Our arms melded, our forms twisting sideways. Then we were landing half on, half off the exact catwalk I'd been aiming toward.

Or make that Kira three-quarters on and me three-quarters off the unyielding metal. "Don't fall!" my sister cried, clutching at my shoulders as I slid over the edge until only fingertips kept me aloft.

And, with a pop of returning air, vision that had narrowed into catwalk-sister-catwalk expanded back out to include the rest of the world. Snow blew in a broken window, the metal platform vibrated beneath me, and twenty feet below the world erupted into snaps and snarls of a dozen werewolves at least.

I couldn't afford to glance down, though. Not when Kira was clinging to my arms while the sway of the catwalk suggested someone rushed upward to finish the job gravity and overconfidence had begun. Clawing against the metal, I attempted to drag myself back onto the horizontal surface. After all, if I lost my nerve and my grip, who would keep my sister safe?

A broken fingernail sent a streak of agony shuddering up my spine as gravity stretched fingers closer and closer to the edge of the metal. Now I was clinging by one and a half hands only, the pain of ripped keratin causing two fingers to slip loose.

Meanwhile, the shouts from below had grown louder, as if I was already falling toward the pitched battle beneath my feet. I wasn't going to be able to chin my way back onto the catwalk, I realized. Not from this awkward angle more beneath than to one side of the surface I was attempting to attain.

"Stand back, Kira," I gritted out as my sister once again tried to help me rise and nearly toppled over the edge in the process. If I fell, I'd shift to fox form and survive, damn the consequences. On the other hand, if Kira fell then this entire rescue would have been for naught. I knew which scenario I preferred.

Of course, my sister was a pro at ignoring things she didn't want to hear. Laying down on her belly, she managed to reach all the way under my armpits this time. "You're not falling," Kira proclaimed, her voice angry even though a stream of tears dripped from both eyes to plop onto my chin.

"Kira, I'm serious," I started. "It's not going to kill me...."

And then Crow was there behind her. Was pushing my sister aside as he lifted me back onto the catwalk as easily as if I was a child. "Come," the werewolf told us, not even out of breath as he lashed out to grip both me and Kira by one arm apiece.

The hand in question latched down with predictable werewolf firmness...then Crow's fingers twitched away as if the ability to become a fox was somehow contagious and likely to rub off on him. The male eventually forced himself to regain his grip, but I took advantage of the lapse in order to glance below.

As earlier sounds had suggested, the theater was now filled to the brim with shifters, some in human and some in lupine form. There were so many that they'd pushed the building's earlier occupants out of the aisle and onto the stage then surrounded Gunner and his compatriots within a nearly seamless wall of human hands and lupine teeth. Still, despite the milling mass of movement, my eye was immediately drawn to the four small figures who had watched in horror as I shifted several moments before.

Ransom, Tank, Allen...and Gunner, whose earlier bruises were now hidden beneath streams of blood running down his arms and face.

Just as in the Arena, my employer was intent upon protecting his brother at his own expense. Unfortunately, this wasn't a battle to first blood. Instead, as I watched far-too-familiar werewolves attack in a badly coordinated yet still overwhelming wave, I winced at the growing carnage beneath my feet.

Jackal's not-quite-pack had found us. And they seemed intent upon taking Gunner and his brother down.

I SHOULD HAVE CHEERED at the realization that most of the males who knew my secret were floundering beneath enemy attack. But, instead, I ripped myself out of Crow's still-lax handhold, assessing my options as I backed away from my captor's advance.

There were two ladders extending down from this particular section of the catwalk, I noted. The one Crow had been pulling us toward led left toward a rear entrance currently devoid of battling shifters. The other led right directly into the heart of the melee.

My fox nature suggested that turning left was a fine idea. Flee, protect my sister, and live to fight another day.

But I couldn't tear my eyes away from Gunner, who was now grunting out a muddled combination of battle rage and breathless agony. And no wonder since two wolves were latched onto his ankles while a human-form shifter layered punch after punch upon the alpha's unprotected chest and neck. Gunner was putting every ounce of energy he had into shielding his brother, which meant his own body was taking a beating even a werewolf couldn't stand up against for long.

It was four against approximately four million. And Kira was safe, Crow's arm encircling the girl's shoulders not to restrain her motion but rather to ensure the girl wouldn't tumble over the edge of the catwalk should she lose her footing on the descent.

For a split second, I couldn't understand why Crow thought touching me was akin to picking up dung with his bare hands while Kira was a porcelain doll in need of protection. Then I remembered that no one had seen my sister shifting. That given her lack of a star ball, Kira wouldn't be showing off her fox form in the near future either. Surely a pack of boy scouts wouldn't let an innocent twelve-year-old come to harm....

So I chose the un-fox-like path of helping the precise male slated to execute me. Chose the right ladder instead of the left.

"Wait, I'm coming with you!" Kira cried, properly assessing my decision one instant before my feet began to move.

But she was currently safe and Gunner wasn't. So sprinting toward the proper ladder, I slid down the rungs like a firefighter and landed directly in the heart of the melee.

Chapter 33

I was vastly outnumbered, but I'd also brought a sword to a wolf fight. No wonder the furry bodies parted before me like so many rabbits fleeing from a sharp-taloned hawk.

Unfortunately, I'd left my clothes up on that catwalk, and wolf teeth are quite effective against unprotected human flesh. Fangs clamped down around my ankle one instant before I whirled and sliced a gash along the biter's hipbone. And even though he released me with a yelp, I could feel the blood puddling atop my foot as I continued on my path.

The pain was minimal, though, compared to the agony of those before me. Because I could still see Ransom and Gunner, their heads barely visible across the sea of two-legged and four-legged opponents who had them so badly outmatched. Allen and Tank must have both donned their animal shapes for protection, but their pack leaders stood tall above the others...or as tall as they could be while fighting off dozens of werewolves with what appeared to be the a pipe wrench and the leg of a wooden chair.

They weren't just outnumbered; they were drowning. No wonder Ransom's left arm hung limply against his side while Gunner appeared to be favoring his opposite leg. I redoubled my efforts to reach them, pushing forward one slow step at a time even as I kept my ears open for any hint that Kira wasn't making good on her escape.

Slice and stab, duck and lunge. At first, only the closest members of Jackal's pack had realized I existed. But now half a dozen enemies peeled away from the Atwood brothers, arrowing directly for me instead. *"Spilt water will not return to the tray,"* Mama noted unhelpfully, breaking into my realization that coming down here by my lonesome hadn't been the brightest idea after all.

We were losing. Of course my sword wasn't enough to make up for a horde of enemies. Ransom bellowed as a wolf broke through his brother's defenses, an agonizing scream sounded far too much like it had come from Allen's lips, and I was still too distant to make any difference in the end game that was about to go down....

But then the front doors were flung wide open and twice as many werewolves entered with Tank at the head of the charge. So the rough-featured shifter hadn't gone lupine. He'd instead fled to rustle up far more backup than I'd thought the Atwood brothers had waiting on their beck and call.

And just like that, the tide shifted. Now it was the Atwood pack who outnumbered the enemy. Meanwhile, the newcomers were also better trained in working together, their force splitting seamlessly into two groups that looped around the perimeter of the stage area while a third arrowed directly toward their bosses in the center of the action.

"And I guess I'm not needed here anymore," I murmured, leaping up onto a piece of stage furniture that had been left behind after the theater's final production. I'd avoided the high ground previously because it led away from the center of action rather than toward it. But Gunner didn't appear to need me after all....

Before relief could relax tensed muscles, though, the floor shuddered beneath my feet as something huge thundered into the outside of the building. A quieter clink of metal against tiles sent my head swiveling in yet another direction, then smoke erupted at floor level as black-clad figures raced in through every entrance point.

Wolves and two-leggers alike gagged and yelled in confusion as a gas-masked human emerged from the haze. "Call off your dogs and come out with your hands up!" the spokesman demanded, his words expanding out from a bullhorn to take over the entire space. "This is the police. You're all under arrest."

BOTH FOLLOWERS OF JACKAL and of the Atwoods fell to the ground without regard to alliances, hacking and coughing as tear gas broke through the battle fervor that had previously held them in its grip. Luckily, the air was clearer atop the scuffed table. So I held my breath, leapt, and barely managed to land on the closest ladder as police in riot gear streamed in every door.

"Stand down!" Gunner called across the roiling mass of mist and bodies beneath me, his voice breaking off into a desperate coughing fit halfway through the final word. But the simple knowledge that the alpha was well enough to give orders spurred my footsteps, and I managed to reach catwalk level before being forced to inhale a breath of my own.

Up here, the air was just barely breathable...and my sister, I noted was still very much present rather than having been rustled out the back door as I'd hoped she would have been. "They're fine," she told me, pointing toward the center of the battlefield where Gunner and Ransom were currently being cuffed and frog-marched out along with all the other two-legged shifters.

Unfortunately, Kira's reassurance hadn't reached only my own ears. "There's the kid!" a cop yelled from beneath us. And while his words really should have been lost amid the whines of teary-eyed werewolves, several other officials peered upwards as he spoke and moved to join in the charge.

Meanwhile, next to the wide-open front door, one tall, lean figure pushed through the sea of ailing werewolves toward us. I tried to tell myself this was just another police officer heeding the call of his compatriots, but the male's excessive height and skinny frame provoked the sinking suspicion that Kira's social worker had caught up with us at last.

It was time to get the hell out of there. But even though I turned in a frantic circle, I found no windows through which we could escape. No doors had been left unbarricaded either. And each ladder now had multiple cops streaming up its rungs.

"The bamboo that bends is stronger than the oak that resists," Mama murmured. Bending? She probably meant not only surrendering but also appearing human. So, sucking in my breath, I relinquished my weapon and donned clothes the magical way, transforming myself from naked warrior into no-really-I'm-just-an-average-civilian as quickly as I could.

Beside me, Crow's eyes widened as my weapon poofed into nonexistence. Then his fists clenched as thin filaments of magic streamed across my skin before coalescing into a cream-colored garment that might have been overlooked from ten or twenty feet away.

Up close, though, the effect was in no way overlookable. Crow had been sent to watch over me and Kira, but I could tell he was now second-guessing the decision to help me back up onto the catwalk rather than pushing me off its edge earlier. What his alpha would do when Crow reported my lapses remained to be seen....

Then the police were ripping Kira away from us, were slamming me and Crow face down into the catwalk and snapping handcuffs around our wrists. "You have the right to remain silent. Anything you say can and will be held against you in a court of law."

Too bad Gunner's mild-mannered cousin wasn't present this time to talk us out of our current predicament.

Chapter 34

We reconvened on the pavement outside, policemen working their way through the crowd and handing out tickets right and left. There was no way to take all of us into custody, but I figured we'd each end up with hefty fines. The lucky combatants were the ones who'd remained four-legged and were released into the custody of a supposed "owner" with no more than a pat on the head.

I, on the other hand, wasn't so fortunate. "What were you trying to do with the child?" one policeman demanded, wrenching me back around to face him when all I wanted was to enfold my sister in yet another well-earned hug. Kira hadn't been wearing either a coat or hat when she was taken yesterday, and I didn't like the way her teeth were chattering now.

"I'm her guardian," I countered...then paused as the same lanky figure I'd seen earlier stalked toward me out of the crowd. Sure enough, when the male ripped off his gas mask, the social worker I'd eluded one day prior emerged from behind the covering.

"You *were* her guardian," Simon countered. "No longer. I'm taking Kira into protective custody."

"But..." I started, only to be cut off once again, this time by the sound of a shifter's voice emerging from behind my back.

"You're taking a child away from her only living family? For what reason, may I ask?"

I turned, half expecting Liam to have arrived after all. But, instead, Tank stalked forward, looking no more prepossessing than he had when I saw him last. The male's nose had been broken then reset improperly many years earlier, his eyebrows fuzzed upward to take over half his forehead, and he weighed more than both the cop and the social worker combined. Despite those facts, however, the male's voice was urbane as he pushed his way into our little grouping, placing one hand possessively upon my back.

"Who are you?" Simon demanded, attempting to separate me from the intruding werewolf. Tank was approximately as movable as a brick wall, however, so the social worker had little luck tearing us apart.

"Ms. Fairchild's lawyer," Tank answered easily. He pulled out his billfold, removed a card that did, indeed, list his job title as "Attorney-at-law." The paper was heavily textured, the letters gold-embossed and well-scripted, and I could see the cop measuring up the likelihood of ending up on the wrong side of a civil case...and finding the odds not at all to his liking. Perhaps that's why the uniformed officer took one huge step backward, leaving me alone with the social worker and the wolf.

Unfortunately, Simon was less easily intimidated. Sometime between last night and this morning, he'd apparently decided that I was an unfit guardian for a child, and he wasn't any more willing to back down now. "Social services has the right to withdraw any foster child from temporary custody without notice," he started.

"And Ms. Fairchild has the right to sue your ass back into the Stone Age," Tank replied. This time, I could smell the waves of fury radiating off the male shifter, and I wasn't surprised when Simon's fight-or-flight instincts kicked in at last. After all, humans might not be aware of the existence of were-wolves...but their lizard brains knew how to protect their own skins.

"I'll be bringing this matter to my supervisor's attention," Simon said after one long moment of loaded silence, snatching the business card out from between Tank's extended fingers. But he didn't argue the matter further. Just stalked away, leaving me alone with yet another werewolf who'd recently seen me shift into vulpine form.

LUCKILY FOR THE SAKE of my skin, Tank seemed even less interested in my secrets than Crow had been earlier. So instead of tearing into me verbally, the male left without another word, fancy business cards spreading through the crowd like confetti as he squared away matters with officer after officer until every Atwood wolf had been released from custody.

Which left me to warm up my chilled sister...who, I belatedly realized, was no longer hovering by my side. I vaguely recalled an EMT pulling Kira away to check her vitals a few minutes earlier. But now the tween was invisible, lost within the milling crowd.

And the number of bystanders appeared to be growing larger by the minute. I didn't recognize even half the faces around me, suggesting that Ransom's backup forces had been even more extensive than they'd appeared from my elevated perch in the theater. No wonder Jackal stuffed his driver's license back into his wallet after a policemen relinquished the rectangle of plastic, glaring at me only once before leading his underlings stiff-leggedly away into the snow.

I had little interest in future battles, though. Instead, I pushed between rock-hard shifters, searching for a sister who resolutely refused to be found. "Kira!" I called, not wanting to bring any more attention to myself than was absolutely necessary but driven to desperation by the absence of a sister who had disappeared without a trace only a day before.

I smelled her before I saw her. Caught a hint of caramelized sugar seconds before a raised hand waving in my direction from the other side of the street. "I'm fine!" Kira told me, voice filled with just as much wounded dignity as if I'd forgotten her age and had warned her to look both ways before crossing the street in front of her sixth-grade compatriots.

And despite everything, my lips curled upward in response. Kira was the ultimate tween, certain of her own abilities and craving independence. I loved the fact that even dangling from a rope in an abandoned theater hadn't robbed her of that trait.

Unfortunately, my own resilience wasn't through being tested. Because the search for my sister had drawn the exact sort of attention I'd been hoping to avoid.

"Mai." My name slid across the crowd like a snake stalking its dinner. And I was pretty sure that in this scenario, I was the featherless baby bird.

Chapter 35

Unwillingly, I turned away from Kira and sought out the alpha who had watched me shift less than an hour earlier. Gunner must have heard Crow's side of the story already, must be rewriting all of our past interactions in light of recent events....

Only, it wasn't just Gunner glowering at me from across the thinning gathering. Instead, both siblings stood shoulder to shoulder, their features so similar a stranger might have found it hard to tell them apart.

To me, though, the males were night-and-day different. Because Ransom's eyes were filled with amusement—had he somehow missed my fox fur party before all hell broke loose? Gunner, on the other hand, boasted muscles clenched so tightly I was pretty sure nobody would have been able to pull the stick out of his ass.

"Come here," Gunner growled once he saw he'd gotten my attention. And to my despair, my feet began moving in his direction no matter how hard I fought the impulse with my rational mind. It was the debt, I realized. The dragon of an owing that I'd willingly allowed to sink its claws into my flesh while Kira was caught in the grasp of someone who'd already murdered two innocents at least.

The more I fought, though, the more control slipped through my fingers. So I wasn't even able to glance sideways by the time we three settled beneath an awning and out of the snow. Instead, I peered straight ahead, noting that the huge male bodies raising my heart rate also blocked the entrance to a pawnshop. Unfortunately, it was far past closing time. So no one came out to drive the werewolves away and set me free.

"Well," Ransom said at last, breaking the silence after we'd stood there for several long seconds, nothing but white breath flowing between us in the cold. "A fox."

He paused, and for the space of one hopeful breath I thought maybe the local pack leader didn't know whatever secrets made bearing star-ball magic so dangerous for me and my kin. After all, I wasn't privy to that information. Why should a werewolf be more knowledgeable about my own heritage than I was?

But then he continued: "A kitsune. An offense punishable by death."

"My sister isn't like me," I started, lying about the one thing that truly mattered. My own fate had already hardened into certainty, but I could at least ensure Kira slipped out from beneath the descending ton of bricks before they landed on her head. "We're half-sisters. Same mother, different fathers...."

"...strange, then that fox nature travels down through the mother's line." Ransom smiled at me then, his teeth so sharp they gleamed despite the gray of incipient snowfall. He'd apparently researched this subject, or perhaps had been raised to hunt foxes at his father's knee.

Wherever Ransom's savvy came from, it was clearly bad news for me and Kira. And my first impulse, as always, was to count on fox agility to ensure my escape. To run through the crowd and snatch my sister then flee together until both At-wood brothers faded into a vague memory from our past.

But the debt didn't let me twitch a single muscle away from my current companions. And now Gunner was sliding closer to back up his sibling, fist clenched and brow lowered as pure aggression radiated off his skin.

ONLY, GUNNER DIDN'T face me when he finally interjected himself into the conversation. Instead, his shoulder slid between me and his brother, making promises that contradicted his unwillingness to meet my eye. "I'll take care of this."

"Hmm, yes, I do believe you will." Ransom had appeared to possess a weak underbelly in the Arena, where his brother persisted in protecting him at every turn. But now I began second-guessing the notion that Ransom was the underdog. Because the elder sibling appeared plenty authoritative at the moment, his mere presence making it difficult for me to breathe. "If you don't want me to deal with these two kitsune in the traditional manner," he informed his brother, "then you'll keep them far away from the heart of our pack."

"Of course." Gunner pushed himself further between me and the pack leader as he spoke, the wall of flesh allowing me to suck in a much-needed lungful of air. "I'll make sure they do no damage..."

"...And you'll keep an eye on them *personally*."

"Brother?" Gunner's question was careful, his eyes averted so far I could make out the pained crinkling above his cheekbones. This level of submission was traditional when speaking to a stronger werewolf, but I'd always gotten the impression that power flowed in the opposite direction between the two brothers.

Apparently I'd been wrong about a lot.

"Let me be more clear." Now I could once again smell the fur of Ransom's presence, could see the older male's eyes piercing me over his brother's shoulder as he stepped up into Gunner's personal space. "I'm done being mollycoddled. You're not the pack leader. I am. And now you'll take one huge step backwards as I stand in my rightful place at the head of the clan."

"Of course you're the pack leader." I could have told Gunner that such a placating tone wouldn't work against his brother. But apparently the younger alpha felt the need to at least try.

"*Silence.*" Whether or not Ransom was powerful enough to make that command stick, the male between us subsided instantly. And we both listened as the Atwood pack leader laid down the law. "You'll stay here until I call for you. No more manipulations to avert my orders. No more undermining my commands."

"Yes, Chief." Gunner's head bowed in acceptance. But his fists clenched when his brother refused to accept a simple affirmative.

"You'll swear it."

I kept expecting Gunner to sell me out, to decide that Kira and I weren't worthy of such a severe loss of face. But, instead, he dropped down onto one knee in the slush of snow melt without hesitation, the ice that currently froze my toes surely sliding through his clothes to bite at his skin as well.

But Gunner's feet were warmer than mine, metaphorically at least. Because he spoke so clearly that even I could feel the magic imbuing his promise. "I swear to obey you, brother, in this as in all things. From this moment forward, I am your man."

"Good," Ransom answered. Then, without a hint of compassion for the profound concession he'd dragged out of his sibling, he turned on his heel and left us both alone.

Chapter 36

Gunner's ensuing silence was oppressive, but I had more important matters on my mind than a glowering alpha's injured pride. Matters like Kira, whose facade of spunky indifference faded the instant the last police officer rolled away in his patrol car, leaving us alone with one painfully silent alpha and the three pack mates who'd chosen self-imposed exile over returning to the heart of their clan.

"Let's go home," I suggested, taking in the way my sister's lower lip was beginning to quiver while the arm I'd slung around her waist did most of the work of holding the girl upright. Kira sagged in silent acceptance of my game plan, and I hugged her tighter in lieu of wrapping the shivering child in the jacket I no longer possessed.

Meanwhile, I glanced over Kira's shoulder at the boarded-up theater. The owner had finally arrived to lock the doors and cover broken windows, so there was no slipping inside now to grab the possessions I'd left on the catwalk. Plus, the officer in charge had warned us to get moving, the glint in his eye suggesting he'd be driving back around in a few short minutes to make sure everyone had dispersed.

So—back to our apartment, where Kira could snuggle up under the covers and I could change into non-magical garb.

Unfortunately, my companions weren't impressed by my proposed retreat.

"Not a good idea," Crow offered before kneeling down to assess Allen's injuries. The accountant perching on the curb below us hadn't been one of the two males who'd died in wolf form this evening, but he hadn't come through the battle unscathed either. Instead, he hissed as Crow rolled up his left pant leg, the swelling and mottling above Allen's knee suggested he'd either broken a bone or pulled something serious on the inside.

"Yeah, stupid to go back where Kira's kidnapper can find her so easily," Tank agreed, glowering at me from under lowered brows as he joined his pack mates in the snow. Then, turning his attention to Allen, he added, "This is going to hurt" one second before wrenching the accountant's swollen leg back into place.

So, a displaced bone rather than a broken one. I pressed Kira's nose into my neck, covering her ears with my hands in an effort to cut off Allen's agonizing scream. "You could have at least offered him a sip of whiskey," I growled at the lawyer-turned-medic, surprising myself with how much Allen's pain had cut into my gut.

But werewolves were resilient. Allen offered me a reassuring smile at the same time Gunner finally reentered the conversation, stalking over to join us after seeing the last of his brother's men off. "Mai and Kira will come home with us," the alpha stated, proving that he hadn't missed our conversation even though he'd been talking to someone else a dozen yards away. With the effortless grace of a predator, he pulled Allen upright, draped a jacket around Kira's shoulders, then turned in the direction of the SUV without bothering to wait for our reply.

And I should have argued. Should have asserted my independence. But I was bone weary, any confidence that I could protect Kira on my own thoroughly shaken by recent events.

So we went. Accepted two bedrooms on the second story of the mansion—although the wrinkling of Kira's brow foreshadowed the moment five minutes later when she snuck back down the hall to bunk with me. The two of us listened to computerized gunfire emanating from the far end of the hallway where the guys were winding down to the tune of a highly violent video game, then we allowed our eyelids to gradually lower into sleep.

When I woke, five minutes or five hours later, the mansion was silent around us, my skin cold against the late-night air. Kira had rolled sideways and pulled the blankets along with her, but it wasn't just lack of bedding that sent goosebumps shivering across my skin.

The laptop. In the relief of surviving a pitched battle and police standoff, I'd forgotten the serial killer's MO. Had assumed that whoever initially wanted my sister was now gone without a trace, a few hours of shuteye making no difference to our own search.

But our opponent was a cat-like predator, one who enjoyed playing with his prey. Why else dangle Kira so theatrically when he could have simply tortured any secrets out of her? Why lure me in with a note on my door rather than snatching me off the street?

And what would a cat do when partially successful but cheated of the full prize he thought he deserved? He'd wait and hope the mouse would crawl back into the trap so he could snap the jaws the rest of the way shut.

I wasn't a mouse, though. I was a fox. And if I got to that laptop while the killer was still connected, perhaps I could use his own cockiness to figure out exactly who he was.

Chapter 37

I slipped out of bed silently, pulling on the baggy jogging outfit Allen had lent me in lieu of absent clothing of my own. Even though the accountant was the smallest of the werewolves living in this mansion, I could barely draw the string tight enough to keep the pants up around my waist. But at least I'd stay warm this time around...and could carry my star ball in the far more useful form of a sword.

I didn't leave immediately, though. Instead, I hovered over Kira, loathe to be away from her for even an hour. Not that I thought someone would sneak into the mansion and snatch the child while she was sleeping. Our enemy didn't seem idiotic enough to break into an alpha werewolf's lair while Gunner was in residence. Still, if my sister woke and guessed where I'd gone off to...well, experience proved she'd dive into the fray without bothering to look before she leapt.

It was the cold of floorboards chilling my bare feet that suggested the solution to that particular conundrum. Sneakers. I needed shoes anyway if I was going to walk through the city two-legged, and surely even Kira would turn back to the warmth of the mansion the moment her toes froze into blocks of ice.

My feet were half an inch longer than Kira's, but I managed to stuff them into my sister's shoes anyway. Then I was gone, out the door, through the hallway, sliding down the banister in a burst of joy at the unfettered freedom I'd wrapped around myself.

Because Kira was safe and I was finally going on the offensive rather than acting like a night-blind chicken fleeing a fox in the hen house. *I* was the fox this time. And I was ready to hunt.

But my mother's ghost wasn't so sure. *"Stepping into a melon field, standing under a plum tree,"* she warned me, her words so adamant that I turned in a circle to make sure she wasn't actually present. But, no, I was alone in the entranceway of the mansion, only five feet distant from the freedom represented by the gargantuan front door.

Unfortunately, I remembered this particular proverb from my childhood. Remembered how I'd argued that I wasn't stealing sweets when Mama came in and found me with my hand literally stuck in the cookie jar at five years old. Gunner would judge my actions similarly if he woke in the night and found my bed empty save for Kira. I wasn't running away this time...but how was he to know that?

The resultant twinge of guilt—plus something far less identifiable—sent me creeping back up the same stairs I'd recently slid down, continuing to backtrack until I hovered indecisively outside the alpha's bedroom door. Something about this moment felt like a turning point. Like an admission that I no longer hunted solo, that I needed someone to watch my back.

That thought nearly sent me scurrying back in the opposite direction as fast as my legs would carry me. But I needed to be rational here. Needed to remember that there was more at stake than my fox-sensitive pride. Ensuring I captured our opponent rather than being captured by him was more important than asserting prickly independence when Kira was the one who'd suffer if I failed.

So I didn't flee. Still, I turned the doorknob thief-in-the-dark slowly, not quite willing to commit to this path by waking Gunner up. And...he heard me anyway. Heard and was across the room before I'd caught more than the barest hint of movement out of the dark.

"I was wondering if you'd leave without me," the alpha rumbled. And when he smiled, I caught a glimpse of wickedly pointed, wolf-sharp teeth.

I MUST HAVE SQUEAKED, because Gunner stepped backwards, cold air rushing in to cool my suddenly heated cheeks. And as he moved, the moonlight played across his bare chest, sliding over muscles that my fingers suddenly itched to stroke.

So *that's* why my subconscious had been strangely willing for me to accept a hunting partner. Apparently my instinctive side wanted to do more than *hunt* with this wolf.

Dropping my eyes, I clenched my hand over the hilt of my sword but found little comfort in the cold weight beneath my fingers. A bladed weapon wasn't going to cut through the confusion and embarrassment that now rioted beneath my skin.

As if sensing my discomfort, Gunner's chuckle rolled over me like a warm-fingered caress, so different from the cold silence with which we'd parted earlier in the evening. "I'll put on clothes if that'll make you feel better," he offered, his voice receding into the darkness. And my feet followed after him without consideration for the self-preservation instinct that should have made me wait out in the hall.

Gunner's bedroom smelled like a jungle. Like male and power and seduction wrapped up in the crispness of fresh dew on pine needles. "I remembered the laptop," I called into the silence, hating the fact that I had to clear my throat halfway through my first sentence to ensure the rest of the words came out clear. "It's a long shot, but Kira's kidnapper might still be linked to it. He was talking to Kira through the speakers when I showed up."

"He?" And Gunner's attention was trained once again upon the mystery, the almost tangible sway he'd held over my body receding as quickly as it had begun. I was disappointed in myself for regretting the absence, which might explain why I offered more information than my companion had really asked for.

"It was a computerized voice," I answered, catching a glimpse of hard muscles rippling across Gunner's abdomen as he pulled a shirt on over his head. "Anonymous. But, yes, my gut says it was a he."

"Speaking in real time?"

"Do you really still think the killer is your brother?" I countered, attention finally snagged by the puzzling dynamics flowing between the two males. "Ransom was fighting by your side against Jackal's wolves yesterday. He let you take charge of me and Kira without batting an eye."

For a moment, I thought I'd pushed too hard. Because the granite of Gunner's aroma rose up to overtake the fresh, leafy odor, and he sank down onto the bed to lace up his boots without bothering with a reply.

But then Gunner laughed out a short "Heh" beneath his breath, glancing up at me with an almost hangdog droop to his features. "I'm still figuring out my brother," he answered, the words coming slowly as if they were just now coalescing for the very first time.

For my part, it was dawning upon me that this alpha's earlier silent treatment hadn't been anger at my actions. Gunner's instinct outside the theater had been to protect me...which had likely confused him as much as it did everybody else. So I hummed out a question, gave my companion the space to speak or not as he saw fit.

"When we were kids, Ransom was the rash one," Gunner continued after a long moment. "He made...mistakes...and was glad to have me as his compass. But maybe he's grown out of that. Maybe he doesn't need me any longer."

The pain in Gunner's voice was palpable, so I did my best to brush his worries aside. "Siblings always need one another," I countered, unable to imagine a day when Kira and I would be glad to see the other's taillights receding in our respective rear-view mirrors.

"Well," Gunner answered, neither overtly agreeing nor disagreeing. He was fully dressed now, cloth covering every delectable surface before I'd had a chance to really see any of it in the light. "Are you ready? We're less likely to wake the household if we go out the back."

Chapter 38

The snow had nearly melted by the time our headlights swept across the face of the abandoned theater, illuminating the marquee. *The Importance of Being Earnest.* Were even long-ago playwrights giving me tips on how to live my life now?

"I brought a crowbar," Gunner started, then swore beneath his breath as a police cruiser came toward us from the opposite direction. I'd never known the cops to have such a presence in the Warren, but perhaps they figured an event serious enough to make the local papers merited a follow up visit...or three.

So we couldn't park out front as originally intended. Instead, we continued past our destination and waited to pull into a side alley once the police car was long out of sight. We hugged the shadows, walking like octogenarians on the way back as the previous evening's tight muscles and scabbed-over wounds hindered our progress. But aches and pains were forgotten when Gunner slipped his crowbar under the edge of a board-covered window, prompting me to stop him with one hand lightly touching his arm.

"That's going to be crazy loud," I protested, remembering the awful screech of a pried-up nail the one time I'd tried—and failed—to make our shabby apartment a little bit spiffier.

"Alternatives?" Gunner countered, cocking his head and waiting for me to come up with another way in.

Rather than answering, I tilted my chin to gaze at the barely-visible stars, trying to remember when I'd started telling alpha werewolves what to do. And as I forcibly relaxed my neck muscles, I caught a square of darkness in the third story, a broken window too high for the owner to have bothered boarding up.

"Look." I pointed upward, only realizing as I did so that neither a human nor a wolf would have even considered making such a climb.

But Gunner had already seen firsthand what I was able to shift into. So I ignored decades of conditioning and spoke openly about my secret for the very first time. "It'll be easy to get up there as a fox. Then I'll come downstairs and let you in."

I expected Gunner to growl at the overtness of my offer. But, instead, his voice was almost too level to be natural as he answered me after a short pause. "You'll fall."

"I won't. The climb is easy. Especially if you give me a boost onto that ledge."

There was something flowing between us that I couldn't quite put my finger on, and I held my breath waiting for the other shoe to drop. But instead of acting the way I'd always been told werewolves would respond to my foxishness, the alpha merely waved one hand. "Be my guest."

Which is when I remembered the prerequisite for donning red fur. Getting naked. Right here in front of Gunner, with no other eyes present to depersonalize the effect.

It took three throat clearings before I managed to spit out the solution. "Turn around," I demanded.

Gunner was amused, I could smell that in the air between us. Still, he obeyed me, and I quickly slid out of Allen's jogging suit and Kira's sneakers before assuming my animal form.

Only then did I realize my companion had been peeking. Caught the glint of his eyes skimming across my completely un-wolf-like fur and body. The contact was nearly tangible in its intensity....

But Gunner didn't growl or move to attack. Instead the big, scary alpha werewolf got down on one knee and offered his left arm as a ramp leading up onto his shoulder. "Come on. I'll give you a leg up."

I SLIPPED THROUGH THE window as easily as if I spent hours every day four-legged rather than donning my fur once every other blue moon. No wonder Kira seized every opportunity to frolic as a fox. Light-assisting vulpine pupils made it a breeze to scamper through the upper story in near darkness, and I barely managed to force myself back into human form upon reaching the closed door at the top of the stairs.

Thumbs, I reminded myself. *Doorknobs require thumbs.*

Shivering out of my fur, I came to stand two-legged atop the rough floorboards. And, at first, I thought the goose bumps breaking out on my skin were the result of unheated air brushing up against abruptly furless skin.

But my seldom-utilized animal nature refused to go back to sleep now that it had been wakened. And the stairs yawned dark and cavernous before my dilated eyes.

Shaking off the strange case of the willies, I tiptoed down without calling upon my star ball for illumination. There was always a slight chance an enemy remained in the building, or that one had returned after the police sweep to mop up curious foxes like myself. Better to stub my toe than to arrive heralded by the glow of a magical flashlight....

Unfortunately, walking blind resulted in more than toe stubbing. I was halfway down the stairs when my heel brushed against soft fur in the darkness. And I'm ashamed to admit I emitted a rather feminine "Eek!" as I leapt a foot into the air.

The mouse—it *was* only a mouse—ran chittering into the darkness. *Get a grip*, I told myself firmly. After multiple police sweeps, the theater was unlikely to house critters larger than a rodent.

So I pushed open the door at the bottom of the stairs at a normal pace and strode directly out onto the back of the stage area. *Huh.* This wasn't where I'd expected to end up when I started down the stairwell. Still, I was here, so I might as well poke around a little. Grab the laptop. Maybe even head up to the catwalk and collect my discarded clothing so I didn't end up facing Gunner a second time in my birthday suit.

But the laptop wasn't present. Instead, the thinnest trickle of sound caught at the edge of my consciousness as I batted aside dusty curtains and got down on my belly to peer at the floor below the stage. I didn't even realize I was hearing something, actually, until I found myself humming along to a tune from both my distant and recent past.

Mama's music box. For the first time all night, my teeth sharpened into the fox equivalent of a werewolf's hunting instinct and I padded silently toward the dressing rooms from which the trail of melody had emerged.

He'd come back. Of course the serial killer hadn't depended upon an anonymous computer voice to make contact. Not when my vulpine curiosity was bound to bring me here before the sun rose....

Which meant I was finally going to get a chance to vanquish Kira's kidnapper, to ensure that my sister never again worried when she walked the streets alone.

There was a light before me now. The flickering glow of a candle visible as I entered the hallway leading to a series of changing rooms. My prey must have grown tired of waiting in the darkness, choosing to camp out in the room at the end of the line. This was almost too easy....

I took one step forward...then spun faster than mere human muscles would have been capable of as I felt the presence of something much larger than a mouse materializing behind my back.

Of course he wasn't waiting by the candle. Any good warrior knows you feint before you attack.

Sure enough, the cloaked figure who arose out of the shadows before me was as anonymous as he was dangerous. His face was hidden beneath a pitch-black hood, the enveloping fabric preventing me from telling anything other than his height—which, as usual, was considerably taller than my own.

But I didn't spend long trying to eke out the being's identity. Because he held in his hand the root of this entire hassle—my mother's star ball converted into a glowing sword.

Chapter 39

"The light distraction was clever," I admitted even as I brought my own magical weapon up into an on-guard position. "But you can't sneak up on a fox."

Predictably, my enemy failed to answer, just lunged forward with speed that proved he was more than human. And even though my well-honed reaction should have been a parry, some instinct told me to twist out of the way instead.

Dodging, unfortunately, wasn't the best move against a sword-wielding opponent. But at least I managed to twist far enough away so his blade snagged a lock of hair rather than slicing through living flesh. And as I pivoted in preparation for the hooded figure's next movement, Mama spoke for the first time in over an hour.

"Even monkeys fall from trees."

"I *am* being careful," I hissed in response, wishing my dead mother would speak plainly and tell me what I was missing here. Was I just jumping at mice when I chose not to engage with my attacker...or was there a real reason not to counter his lunge with my sword?

Unfortunately, I had no time to prod at my mother's ghostly warning. Because my opponent was dancing sideways in a move far too similar to Mama's signature sidle to be coincidence. And I found myself backpedaling rapidly while memories flowed fast and furious through my brain.

The park. My parents. Swordplay and laughter, practice merging into dancing. Dad was straightforward and powerful, light on his feet but not the best feinter if you were familiar with his favorite moves. In contrast, Mama's motions were akin to a leaf dancing along invisible air currents, totally erratic for those of us unable to see the wind.

And this person before me was moving just like Mama had. Was twisting and leaping so mercurially I didn't know where he was going to end up next. Only my vulpine senses helped me dodge a second blow, and this time my enemy's blade flicked sideways just in time to nick my bare hip.

It burned. Not like the usual slice of a blade through muscle; more like running into a flaming torch with the sensitive skin of a cheek or a hand. Was this why both Mama and my gut had both warned me not to touch the stolen star ball? Had Kira's kidnapper tapped into kitsune powers I wasn't even aware of...or was there something deeper at work?

As I pondered, the figure before me drifted sideways, forcing me to pivot to keep him in my sights. Or should that be "her"? Because with the cloak covering my opponent's body, there was no way to tell whether I faced a tall woman or an average-height man. The only visible flesh was long fingers wrapped around the sword hilt, and even those appendages could have belonged to a member of either sex....

Suddenly, I had to know who my opponent was. If Mama's sword bit me again in the process so be it. But I couldn't keep fighting while wondering whether this being might be the parent I thought long dead.

So I went on the offensive. Eyed a folded chair leaning against the wall as I skipped sideways. Then took a running leap, using the top of the chair to fuel my forward motion before pivoting midair to aim toward my opponent's head.

The chair clattered against hard floor tiles. And, vaguely, I noted the sound of a crowbar prying at a window-covering in the distance, the result just as teeth-clenchingly loud as I'd known it would be.

Looked like Gunner had lost patience and decided to break in after all. Not good news with cops patrolling the street.

I didn't possess a single spare breath, though, to suggest that Gunner cool it on the screeching. Because Mama's sword was swiping toward me, proving the error of my original plan.

After all my trajectory had been decided by the way I'd pushed off the wall seconds earlier. No amount of twisting or flailing of my arms now would send me scudding sideways to prevent my opponent's blow from hitting home.

So I did the only thing I could think of. I shifted midair, flickering into my smaller fox form and sliding unharmed under the sword thrust before landing atop my opponent's cloth-covered head.

AS I REGAINED MY EQUILIBRIUM, the sword whizzed past so close that it nearly nicked one of my long red ear tips. Air buffeted, claws dug for traction, and Mama screeched inside my head: *"The broken mirror cannot be made to shine!"*

If I'd possessed human vocal cords, I would have yelled back that it was unhelpful to toss out oblique warnings to someone in the middle of a pitched battle. But, instead, I scrabbled at the fabric beneath my pads, yanking the hood with my teeth then leaping away before my enemy could decide whether it was safe to bring that stolen blade closer to his or her forehead.

And this time, my move was successful. I didn't glance back over my shoulder to peer at my receding enemy, but I could feel the hood fluttering down upon my tail as I darted away. Soon, I'd know exactly who had bought my mother's star ball then paid Ma Scrubbs to have my sister kidnapped....

Unfortunately, my opponent only laughed in reaction to being disrobed. And I could see why as I spun back around, understanding at the same time why the evidence of amusement had come out so muffled and low.

Because my enemy had taken his or her cover-up seriously. Beneath the hood was a black ski mask, the only flashes of humanity revealed by my action being two dark eyes and a tiny circle of a mouth. Meanwhile, I spat out the bitterness of baking soda, understanding why I'd failed to pick up even the barest hint of an odor while standing on my enemy's head.

The laugh itself might have been a clue, but unfortunately I wasn't that lucky. Instead, the low-pitched sound was entirely androgynous even as my opponent continued to chortle beneath his or her breath.

And this time I'd had enough. Jumping upward into humanity, I staggered once due to the speed and frequency of my recent shifts. But then I was screaming out my anger, sword raised as I mimicked a samurai swooping in for the kill.

I was done with caution. It was time to use my skills to take this enemy down.

Chapter 40

"Mai!" Gunner's voice threaded toward me through the otherwise empty building. Vaguely, I noted that my recent yell might have sounded like pain rather than aggression to a distant werewolf. But I could ease the alpha's worries later. For now, I had a fight to win.

Spinning on the balls of my feet, I dodged beneath my opponent's sword, continuing to pretend my only impulse was defense. It wasn't, though. Because I'd stopped worrying about my sword touching my opponent's the moment I lost my temper. Which opened up an endless array of opportunities in the fight ahead.

In the end, I chose the simplest game plan—feigning a stumble in order to bait my cloaked enemy to attack. Predictably, my opponent responded just as I'd expected. He or she easily bypassed my flailing sword arm then lunged toward my left shoulder. All I had to do was wait until the last moment then raise my own weapon in three...two...one....

"*No!*" Mama started, the word perhaps the beginning of a proverb or perhaps her first attempt at giving it to me straight.

And then images flickered behind my eyeballs. Mama on her deathbed, hands shaking as they reached out to fold my much smaller hands around the hilt of a sword so similar to my own. *"This is yours now. Keep it safe until your sister is old enough to understand its power."*

Even though the memory was twelve years old, I still remembered the tingle that ran through me...and the way clinging to Mama's glowing star ball had eased my grief over the months afterwards. Because while my mother's physical body had faded into absence, her spirit had remained beside me for more than a decade. The warm security of her presence had wandered afield to help Kira shift at frequent intervals, but it had always flowed back in my direction whenever I cared to call.

Except the warmth was fading fast now that I actively fought against that beloved connection. The chill began in my feet and quickly engulfed my entire body as I placed my own sword right where it needed to go to slice Mama's star ball violently aside.

I tried to mitigate the offensive at the last moment, understanding too late that magic works on intention first and foremost. I'd launched this attack from a place of rage and hatred, and that might just be enough to finally split my dead mother and me apart.

Which wasn't at all want I wanted. I hoped to cling to the tiny fragment of Mama's undying spirit, to keep her close and listen to pesky proverbs if that was the only way she could communicate from beyond the grave.

But my change of heart came too late. Two thin streams of magical weaponry met for the very first time with a bell-like tone rather than with the usual clang of reverberating metal. And as they did so, an electrical jolt racked my body, the shock hitting me one instant before the connection to my mother's memories winked abruptly out.

I hadn't appreciated what I possessed until it was gone, I now realized. Hadn't appreciated how much I depended upon Mama's silent—and recently not-so-silent—presence to buoy me up. Had I thrust her spirit into the void without a life boat? Or—worse—was she now being forced to empower my opponent, a free spirit turned into a prisoner within the enemy's cloaked form?

No wonder the hooded figure's eyes crinkled with pleasure. No wonder my muscles turned to water even as my opponent's hardened into stone.

The shock at losing a part of myself that I hadn't fully realized was present loosened my grip until it was all I could do to cling onto my sword as I was pushed backward against the wall. I couldn't even struggle. Lacked the presence of mind to duck down and out of my opponent's grasp before being pinned by someone considerably larger and stronger than myself.

I was trapped between a serial killer and a hard place....

Then I was spinning sideways. My neck whiplashed, my limbs flailed in a vain attempt to catch my balance.

And when I came at last to stillness, the back of my skull was pressing hard against the floorboards while I peered up into the panting face of a tremendous male wolf.

Chapter 41

The werewolf's breath was hot against my forehead, his teeth inches away from the soft spot beneath my chin. No wonder I shifted into fox form, depending on animal instinct to wriggle free before I could be eaten alive.

But the wolf was having none of it. He grabbed my newly materialized ruff and shook me so severely my teeth clattered together. And even after I was suitably chastised, the male continued standing stiff-legged atop my crumpled body while a deep growl rumbled up out of his massively broad chest.

Which is about the time I realized this wasn't my sword-wielding opponent. This was Gunner, turned guardian while letting our true quarry escape behind his back. I'd always known alpha werewolves were idiots, but I hadn't expected behavior as ass-backwardly overprotective as this.

Unfortunately, I couldn't shift forms in order to berate him. Not when the reservoir of magic within my belly had gone quiescent with exhaustion, refusing to even create a minor electrical shock to tingle against Gunner's skin. Without Mama's star ball to strengthen me, I apparently had far less stamina than I was accustomed to possessing.

So I lay there panting, unable to so much as twitch without provoking another growl from the alpha straddling my body. Meanwhile, the anonymous being who had paid for my sister's kidnapping after killing two innocent humans disappeared without a trace.

We might have remained stuck in that stalemate all night, too, had a trickle of smoke not emerged from the changing room at the end of the hall. *The candle,* I thought at first, shoulders relaxing back down away from around my ears.

But the stench flowing over us was too foul to have emerged from one small chunk of wax and cotton. Meanwhile, beneath the smoke, I caught the unmistakable scent of gasoline, suggesting our enemy had left us with a parting gift far more serious than one overturned candlestick.

Gunner must have smelled it too because his eyes widened, his signature scent of unyielding granite giving way to the more malleable aroma of ozone and dew. Then my captor became my herder. Nudging me erect then chivvying my footsteps, he pushed me down the hall then out onto the stage proper. And when I veered toward my favorite leather jacket, he hip-bumped me away before literally pushing me out through the unboarded window he'd recently used to enter the building.

In the semi-fresh air of the outdoors, my companion finally managed to shift while I merely dragged my feet a few inches further from the theater that I suspected would soon go up in flames. There was no sign of the conflagration on the exterior just yet, but the building was so very old and built almost entirely out of wood....

"There's a fire," Gunner growled into his cell phone just as the first brilliant streak of orange rose into the barely lit neighborhood. "The theater. Find a burner phone then call 911."

So it was his pack he'd contacted rather than the fire department. *"Clever wolf,"* I mumbled, realizing only after I'd spoken that, of course, I was in vulpine form. So the words came out as a thready whine rather than as understandable human communication.

Gunner didn't look down, but his hand dropped onto my forehead even as his scent hardened further in reaction to whatever his pack mate was relaying over the phone. "The whole apartment?" He paused, listened to something I should have been able to hear in my fox form but couldn't quite manage to focus upon while my body was melting into the watery slush beneath my feet. "And the Ebay account was wiped also?"

Wait, they were talking about *my* apartment and *Kira's* Ebay account. Did that mean the last possible trail leading to our serial killer had iced over during the night?

Forcing myself erect with an effort, I realized only after raising a hand to my aching head that I was standing on two human feet rather than on four furry ones. No wonder I was shivering, the effort of the shift creating a watery haze that obstructed my view.

Those weren't tears, I told myself. Not over a rented space that had formed the bare minimum shelter necessary to keep body and soul together rather than representing any sort of home.

By the time I'd blinked the obstruction out of my eyes, Gunner was already slipping into his clothes and turning off his phone. "Here," my companion told me, pulling Allen's sweatshirt over my head far more gently than I'd thought him capable of before thrusting the matching sweatpants and Kira's shoes into my arms. "We need to make tracks."

So we ran away from the flaming theater together. Fled toward a shiny SUV that promised to carry us to a tremendous mansion nothing like the rat-infested apartment I was used to...and all I really noticed along the way was the fact that the vehicle's heated seats eased a tiny bit of the chill away from my frozen heart.

It would have taken a full-fledged sauna to heat me through at that moment though. And I reached into my mind, hoping for a proverb—*any* proverb—instead of the terrible silence that resolutely filled my brain like a thick blanket of snow. "I think I made a terrible mistake," I murmured, only realizing I'd spoken aloud when Gunner glanced toward me, cocking his head in question.

"Your sister's safe," he offered when my flood of self-recrimination became dammed into silence by the dryness of my throat.

"For now," I countered, voice croaking as I forced further explanation out through parched lips. "But I just gave a serial killer power over my mother's star ball. And if I lose custody of Kira...."

Then a water bottle was being inserted between my trembling fingers, a large hand guiding mine up to tilt the much-needed moisture into my mouth. "You're among wolves now," Gunner promised, the words far less ominous than they would have been one week prior. "Our pack will solve this together."

And even though I'd been trained since birth to catch sight of a werewolf then run in the opposite direction as quickly and stealthily as possible, I believed the words of the alpha beside me. Sank back against the buttery leather seat and relaxed into acceptance.

I was no longer alone. Together, Gunner and I would figure this out.

From the Author

Did you enjoy *Wolf's Bane*? If so, I hope you'll consider taking a moment to leave a review while you wait for *Shadow Wolf*, due to launch in October 2018.

Meanwhile, if you missed it, there are three other series set in this same werewolf world: the Wolf Rampant Trilogy, the Alpha Underground Trilogy, and the Wolf Legacy Quartet. Of these, the first book in the Wolf Rampant series, *Shiftless*, is a great place to start since it's free in ebook form on all retailers.

You can also download a free starter library and explore unique extras when you sign up for my email list at www.aimeeeasterling.com.

Thanks for reading! You are why I write.

15278221R00125

Printed in Great Britain
by Amazon